To Trina
Fuck. on my fac

taboo & tinsel

e. m. moore

E. M. Moore

This book is a work of fiction. Names, characters, places, and incidents are the product of the author's imagination or are used fictitiously. Any resemblance to actual events, or persons, living or dead, is coincidental.

Manufactured in the United States of America
First Edition December 2022

Cover by 2nd Life Designs

Also By E. M. Moore

Warner Bulldog University

The Comeback Pact

The Midseason Fakeout

Rejected Mate Academy

Untamed

Forsaken

Saint Clary's University

Those Heartless Boys

This Fearless Girl

These Reckless Hearts

The Heights Crew Series

Uppercut Princess

Arm Candy Warrior

Beautiful Soldier

Knockout Queen

Finn

Jax

The Ballers of Rockport High Series

Game On

Foul Line

At the Buzzer

Rockstars of Hollywood Hill

Rock On

Spring Hill Blue Series

Free Fall

Catch Me

Ravana Clan Vampires Series

Chosen By Darkness

Into the Darkness

Falling For Darkness

Surrender To Darkness

Coveted by the Dark

Thirst For Her

Ache For Her

Order of the Akasha Series

Stripped (Prequel)

Summoned By Magic

Tempted By Magic

Ravished By Magic

Indulged By Magic

Enraged By Magic

Safe Haven Academy Series

A Sky So Dark

A Dawn So Quiet

one

. . .

THE CITY LIGHTS of Portland reflect off the falling snow, making the flakes glitter as they fall to the icy sidewalk. Red bows adorn tall lampposts. All the shop windows boast some sort of Christmas cheer. Green holly. Painted white snow. Reindeer and Santa. My skin warms underneath my big winter jacket as I search out the pub I Googled only ten minutes prior. It had the best reviews within walking distance of my airport hotel, and after dealing with my heavy course load over the last few months, I deserve a drink. Trust me.

I want to decompress, spend an hour doing no thinking whatsoever. Just enjoy some good food and letting the bite of alcohol dull my mind. It's a weird notion, especially since I'm in my second year of grad school, but sometimes thinking is overrated. Putting the past semester behind me is long overdue, and at least for tonight, I also refuse to think about the possible stress of the upcoming holiday. Tonight is just for me.

Tomorrow is for future Lili's problems, like worrying about her mother meeting an estranged stepbrother for the first time.

Spotting the lit sign up ahead for my destination, I blink snowflakes off my lashes and leave behind the upcoming uncertainty. The heavy wood door to McCallister's groans as I pull it open. According to the 4.4 star rating, this place boasts the best pub food in Portland, something I desperately need after spending the day on planes and in airports with overpriced bottled water and packaged chips.

The smell of fermented beer and good cooking waft around me as I step inside. The toasty interior is like a gentle hug on this cold night. Dim lights and Irish music pouring out of speakers only add to the ambiance. I unwind my scarf from around my neck as I peer around for a spot to sit. The pub is pretty busy for a Wednesday night. A bartender works fast and cheerfully behind a big, cherry wood bar. He grins as I take a seat at an empty stool. "Food or drink?" he asks, moving his stare to fill a pint glass of ale for another customer, the top frothing nicely.

"Both," I answer as I shed my coat and hang it on the back of the stool. Friendly chatter drifts above the music, and before long I have a half-drank Guinness in front of me, the last remaining spoonfuls of a delicious beef stew, and the eye of a gorgeous stranger who's been flirting with me since he sat down.

I forgot what this feels like. The playful banter. The flirting. The squeeze in my stomach as our gazes connect. My nose has been stuck in a book for too long.

It doesn't hurt that this guy is positively electrifying and handsome. He's older than me for sure but it's in more the rugged manliness that piques my attention. His disheveled beard has hints of gray but youthful green eyes spark and burn bright as we talk. A t-shirt and a well-used ballcap top off his appearance which is so different from the guys back on campus. Rough hands wrap around shot after shot as he throws them back. As soon as he finishes one, another appears like magic, and I'm certain he and the bartender have done this before.

Mr. Gorgeous uses his pinky to move a shot into my line of sight. "Now that you've had some food in your belly, take a shot with me."

His deep voice makes my face heat. The tension around us snaps whenever we lock gazes, and the looks he keeps giving me makes me think he feels it too.

He must mistake my momentary silence for indecision because he quickly ribs me. "Come on, don't let an old man drink alone."

I lift a brow. "Old man? Is that what you are?"

His gaze drops, taking me in. "Compared to you." He lingers a little too long on the sparse cleavage I'm showing. It makes me want to go back to the hotel and pull on a revealing shirt to wear tonight, just so his stare would stay longer. "Age comes with some benefits though," he adds, meeting my eyes again.

I lift the shot, and he clinks the one in his hand to

mine. Throwing it back, I try not to react to the burning liquid coating my throat. When the sensation dies down, I ask, "How's that?"

He holds my gaze. "Experience."

The rough texture in his voice has me clenching my thighs. Heat swamps the sensitive area between my legs, a welcome, yet foreign reaction. "Is that so?" I tease, relishing in the feelings just his voice, just this chat is giving me. I have no time to flirt back at school. No time to think about anything other than finishing my degree. If I had a need, I brought out my trusty vibrator before bed and took care of it within a few minutes as if it was a task like doing weekly laundry.

He leans over, his hand coming to rest on my hip while the tips of his fingers edge just under my shirt. As soon as he makes contact with my bare skin, a jolt shoots through me. My breathing grows heavy, and my nipples peak embarrassingly. How long had it been since I'd been touched?

The delicious undertow my body takes almost makes me miss his gruff whisper. "You could find out."

From habit, my mind starts to make plans. If I say yes, where would we do it? What would it be like? Could I—?

No. Tonight is for me, I remind myself. I don't need to think about anything beyond my initial desires. I bite my lip, trying to steady my breaths before I answer, "I'd like to take you up on that."

He squeezes my hip, moving me into him ever so slightly. "Thank fuck, baby girl. I've been staring at these hips all night, and I want them straddled over my face."

I suck in a breath, the heat from before now molten as my panties grow wet with an urgent need.

He pulls back, green eyes flashing as he lifts his hand, signaling for another round of shots. "You need some liquid courage, I bet."

"Who says?" I challenge, gaze dropping to his lips. I watch as he throws back another shot left by the bartender and then drag my stare away from him for long enough to ask for the check.

The bartender shakes his head, gesturing toward my handsome stranger who only scoots another shot in front of me with a wicked grin. "Trust me. I'm older and wiser."

Standing, I wrap my fingers around the shot glass and devour it in a single swallow.

I don't need courage. Far from it. What I need is this man's dangerous mouth on my pussy before I think about all the reasons why I shouldn't.

two

. . .

WE MAKE it as far as his truck.

His hands are all over me. He groans into the night, a cloud of white mist pouring from his mouth as he takes a generous handful of my ass.

"I need you naked," he breathes, his hips grinding into me as he traps me against the cold metal of his truck. His voice is dripping with praise, and even if I had wanted to talk myself out of this, I'm too consumed by him now. "I want to see your pert tits, the pink of that pretty pussy. You've been tempting me all night."

My panties soak straight through. That delicious voice, the way his hands roam… I'm tempted to let him take me against his vehicle, really throwing my cares away.

The parking lot lamp shines down on us as if we're on spotlight though. "Over here, baby girl," he coaxes as he moves me down the truck, his hips still solidly against me so I feel every inch of his rigid erection. And if I go by just that, I know he's packing more than the average guy. Excitement burns through me. Why don't I do this more often? Just fun romps, like a short holiday from the everyday grind.

The back door of his truck creaks as he opens it. Then he lifts me onto the seat, my feet dangling as he works his body between my thighs. He doesn't hesitate in taking a handful of my breasts right over my shirt, his lips searing my collarbone and leaving a wake of heat behind him. "Move back," he orders, and I scoot up the bench seat. The scent of old leather and man greet me as I make my way further into the cab of his truck. He follows after, his solid frame leaning into the front seat to turn on the truck. The engine revs to life as I grab his hips, digging my fingernails into his sides like he did to me inside the pub. His shirt lifts a little, showing off a taut body.

Old man my ass. He's in better shape than… Well, than any guy I've ever been with, actually.

Heat starts pouring from the front vents, and he reaches behind him to close the truck door, encompassing in a private space of our own. Within a few seconds, the lights fade out. I no longer see his eyes that are lost in the shadows of the truck but I feel his penetrating gaze on me anyway. Little by little, my eyesight adjusts, and I nearly gasp at the heady look of lust in his eyes. He's looking at me like I'm sweet enough to eat.

"I need you naked, baby girl," he says again, grasping my coat. I shift so he can take it down my arms, my shirt following shortly after. His plump mouth drops open as I lie back in my black lace bra. My jeans are next, albeit a little more cumbersome to shed but it's amazing what two people can do when they both have the same goal.

Nerves skitter through me as I lie across his seat. "You are perfection," he grinds out, his hand tracing down my stomach to the tops of my panties. My muscles jump underneath his touch. I'm not used to this. Everything he does feels brand new. Forbidden. Much needed excitement pours out of me. My breaths come out harsh and quick as he coaxes me into lifting my ass and then taking my panties off in a slow seduction.

I'm doing this. I'm really doing this.

"You're so wet, you're glistening."

"I might ruin your seats," I hedge as he pushes my legs wide so he can take me all in.

"I'd let you ruin more than that." The moment his gaze meets mine, my heart nearly leaps out of my chest.

We're at a standstill as he devours me with his gaze. Everywhere his eyes focus feels like a physical caress. My pussy throbs in response. "Touch me," I beg. "Please fucking touch me."

He spreads my knees even further, his fingers deftly moving to my clit where he rubs slow circles. I buck into his hand. "Fuck, fuck."

Moaning low in his throat, he keeps his stare on me. "So young. I know I shouldn't." But despite his words, he leans over propping my hips higher so he can trace my clit with the tip of his tongue. I grab the back of his head, a short yelp escaping my throat. I move against him with abandon, threading my fingers through his hair. "You taste like sin," he muses, then moves one hand up my body. "Pull down your bra."

I don't hesitate. I yank the cups down just in time for his fingers to find my nipple. He rolls the tight bud between his fingers before giving it a quick pinch. "Oh God," I breathe, letting the words spill out into the truck. I barely recognize my own voice. It's like I've transformed into some sexual heathen.

There's so much freedom in this. So much like giving the middle finger to all the hell I'd put myself through this year. Already, I'm on the heels of an orgasm due to his expert oral skills. "Please more," I beg.

He pulls away, his hot breath hitting me as he blows out a breath over my starved flesh. "I meant it when I said I wanted you straddling my face, baby girl. I want your juices leaking down my chin. Can you do that for me?"

He brushes the pad of his thumb across my clit as he waits for an answer. Dear God, I would do anything to meet that sweet relief. He starts to maneuver us, giving me no chance but to move with him. I angle out of his way as he lays out on the bench seat. Without giving me a chance to think about it, he grips my leg, moving me over his face, my knees straddling his head.

"It's an even better view from here," he groans before moving my other leg out. I fall on top of him, and he returns to his duty, his tongue tracing my folds, rimming my clit. The noises of pleasure he makes undoes me. I've never done this position with any other guy, but holy shit, I need to remedy that.

His shirt pulls up, and I can't resist moving my hand against his taut stomach, feeling the coarse hairs brush against my palm while he devours me. Beyond that, his jeans are tented, straining. My hands curl into fists as he starts tongue-fucking me. I cry out, this new sensation coating my skin in a sheen despite the crisp temperature outside. The windows are fogged up. My skin is buzzing, and right now, all I can think about is wrapping my lips around this stranger's cock.

I unzip his jeans, forcing them down to reveal the bulge in his boxers. I slip the waistband over his dick, my stomach squeezing when I see the size of him. Shit, he's huge like I thought. "Take it slow," he urges. "Real slow, baby girl."

His words are the opposite of his movements. He's attacking my pussy in the best way, giving it much-needed personal attention. I grip his base, lowering over him. He smells like all man. Husky and the faint traces of leather. I've always been one to reciprocate oral but I'd never much enjoyed giving it. This is different. "Like that, baby girl," he praises as I wrap my lips around him. He bucks into me ever so slightly, and jolt of pleasure rings through me. "Fuck yes, you have beautiful lips." He moans against my pussy as I take him in as far as I can go. With his words and movements, before too long, I'm taking him like a champ.

The only sounds are our hurried breaths, the sounds of sex and pleasure. "Damnit, girl. You like that, don't you? My cock in your hot mouth. Fuck."

I'm running my lips over him without thought, without worrying if he's enjoying himself. It's almost like ravaging a good meal. I don't care if I get it all over my face, I just want every messy, tasty bit.

He grips my ass, his tongue working in and out of me. I groan around his cock. Fuck me. It's happening. "I'm going to," I breathe out, unrestrained.

"Give it to me," he growls. "It's all mine."

I feel the orgasm coming fast and hard. My toes curl. I increase my movements on his cock, pulling him out of my mouth as I scream my pleasure into the air while grinding my pussy against his face when the explosion hits. I can't get enough. I want more and more. And he takes it, working in rhythm with my movements until I shudder the last remaining shockwaves.

My fist still pumping his cock, I don't let up. I move back over him while my waves of bliss subside. I always cared about getting my partner off before but this is something more. A willing mission of accomplishment. I need to make him come.

Arching my back, I move my pussy off his face while I take him down. He cups my breasts as I work my mouth over him. "Just like that. Faster if you can. Fuck. Take me in." Again and again, his praise keeps me swallowing him down so his tip hits the back of my throat. He starts lifting his hips into me at the same time, his movements erratic so I know he's almost there.

His cock jerks, and I almost smile with satisfaction until I feel teeth on my clit.

He nibbles, and I scream as cum shoots into my mouth. He releases my clit a moment later as I swallow his juices. My heart beats a mile a minute, like I've just ran a marathon at top speed. He licks my sensitive bud in a soothing gesture until my juices start pouring again. Moaning, he drinks me up. "Fuck yes."

I breathe out, my gaze lifting to the top of the window where the snow is still falling outside, and goddamn, for two hours at least, I could just be. I could just live.

This stranger doesn't know what a gift he just gave me.

Then a knock sounds on the window…and my heart drops.

three

. . .

I'M ALREADY AWAKE when my alarm starts screaming. Overnight, I'd watched as the ceiling of my hotel room went from shadow to the early days of light streaming in through the big window over the air conditioning unit. Reaching over, I grab my cell off the nightstand and turn off the incessant noise.

The ache in my limbs reminds me of the fun I had last night. It's as if my muscles had been coiled up tight with restraint, and now they're here to tell me I'm still kicking, albeit a little on the sore side.

While I shower, I chuckle as the hot water runs down my body, remembering the heart-dropping moment of hearing the knock on the truck window after we'd used one another. Turns out it was just another couple messing around, but I'd scrambled off my mysterious stranger so quickly like we were going to get caught until the laughter sounded. "Have fun!" a female voice had yelled.

"We're about to do the same ourselves," a male voice called right after. Then the girl yelped in surprise, giggle fading away.

"Shit," I'd breathed, holding my chest like I was going to have a heart attack.

I hold my hand over my chest, remembering the adrenaline coursing through me. I'd burst out laughing, then quickly threw my hand over my mouth. I'd had a fantastic time, but they'd reminded me that I had to go back to the real world. The one where handsome, skilled older men don't drag me into their vehicles and play my body like they'd been doing it all their lives.

Mr. Gorgeous had helped clean me up with his shirt. Maneuvered me around so I could dress again, and then that was it. I barely looked at him as I made my way out of his truck, stretching down to hit the snow-covered parking lot.

When I peered over my shoulder, he had his jeans up, but his top button open. His shirt was still in his hands, and he was smirking after me as I took one last look. Neither one of us made idle promises about contacting the other or doing it again. Hell, I didn't even know his name.

Maybe I am sort of sexual heathen because the fact that I had no idea who this guy was turned me on. Even now, I could just stand here, think about him, and break out the vibrator.

But today was a big day. I didn't have the luxury of time. Still, a part of me wishes I'd gotten contact info from him. I might need a sexy distraction this holiday season. We could have made it a thing while I was in town. Fuck buddies. No strings attached. Just all-out using each other.

After finishing in the shower, I put my makeup on and peer into the mirror. Honestly, if last night taught me anything, it was that letting my hair down from time-to-time is a good idea. Sure, I might not see Mr. Sexy Abs again but that didn't mean I had to go back to my hole of being consumed by school.

I pack my suitcase and then make my way back to the airport via the shuttle. The uncle I've never met before is under the impression I'm getting in today just like Mom and Dad. He'll be here to pick me up. No matter how much I'd tried to arrange so I got here *after* my parents, I couldn't swing it. I'm just going to have to meet him by myself, awkwardness and all.

The only things I know about him are that his name is Cameron Michaels, he used to play for the New England Captains, the professional football team, but he suffered a career-ending injury that made him return home to his father's inn, which he now runs—and until earlier in the year when my Grandma Junie died, I was supposed to hate him. Talk about family drama. My Grandma had a midlife crisis, and in the middle of all that, she'd left my grandfather for another man—Cameron's father. My mom never forgave her. She'd turned down every invitation for holiday get-togethers or meetups, but when Grandma got sick, Mom had a change of heart. It was too late, of course. She never even got to say goodbye, but Grandma wrote her a letter, expressing her wish for her only daughter to get to know her stepson. Now, here we were, about to spend the holidays with a man we don't know, in an unfamiliar town, and in a strange house.

Merry fucking Christmas to me. I'm pretty sure the only real escape I'll get out of this trip happened last night.

The shuttle drops me off at Arrivals, and I walk back in with my luggage like I've just gotten off a plane. Taking up a spot near Baggage Claim, I send a quick text to my mom, telling her I've arrived and am at the airport waiting.

Glancing up, I survey the area, not sure what I should look for. A lonely man standing by himself? Someone with a sign?

A gruff voice sounds behind me. "Did you just get off the flight from Richmond?"

I turn, tucking my phone away, and peer right into a lined piece of paper with my name written on it.

Well, it's kind of my name. I frown at the misspelling. "It's Lilianne with two n's, actually," I say as I look up.

I blink, my heart constricting as the man holding the paper comes into view. It's the stranger from last night. He's clean-shaven now, but there's no mistaking that it's him. He has the same used cap on. Same green eyes.

His face turns white, stricken. "Lilianne?"

"That's me," I tell him, confused. Why is he...? But in the next instant, it hits me.

He's not just my sexy stranger.

He's my uncle, isn't he?

"You're...?"

"I'm..."

Fuck. I sat on my uncle's face.

four

. . .

PART of me still doesn't want to believe it. I just stand there, staring at him. My brain working overtime to try to make something else be true.

How is this possible? The one fucking time I let my hair down. What. The. Actual. Fuck. I should've stayed in my lane. I can do neurotic college student all day, any day, but this...*this*? This I don't know how to do.

He's definitely the same panty-dropping guy from last night, except he doesn't have that sure-of-himself smirk on his face right now. The emotions playing through my mind seem to be going through his too. He's crumpled the last-minute sign with my misspelled name on it in his hands. After a few seconds, it fades, and he just relaxes—somehow—before reaching out his hand, "I'm Cameron—"

"Seriously?" I burst out, trying not to have a panic attack still. "You're introducing yourself to me?"

His jaw hardens. Those beautiful green eyes of his harden. "What the fuck am I supposed to do?"

"I don't know, maybe not tongue fuck your niece?"

My exasperated words are heard by a few passers-by, and I can't even imagine what's going through their minds as they give us a wide berth. "Lower your voice. Fuck," my uncle says, running his hands through his hair as he peeks at the interested onlookers.

Regardless of anything else going on, he's still impossibly good looking. The facial hair is gone but I have the remnants of the beard burn he left between my thighs from eating me out last night…as I sat on his face.

Jesus Christ. I have to stop thinking about that. My skin heats, and it's partly because I'm embarrassed as fuck but it's also due to the memory of the delicious things he did to me. How he made me feel.

He reaches over to take my luggage, but I pull it back. The dark look he gives me silences anything I was about to say. "Your parents are landing in an hour. I thought we would just wait here."

He wrestles the handle away from me and starts rolling it toward the far wall. I have to run to catch up with him because I know he didn't just say something about my Mom and Dad, not with what happened between us. "I can't meet you with my parents. My parents can't come here. They—"

"So, you're going to tell them what? They can't come because you've tasted my cum?" He gives me a doubtful look and then stares off into space. "They're already on their way."

Another wave of heat creeps over me. I open my jacket, fanning the two sides out as my world starts to fall apart. I'm fairly certain my parents still think I'm a virgin. We're not the talk about our feelings and relationships type.

"Here's what we're going to do," my uncle says gruffly.

I hold my hand up to stop him. "It's my parents. I'll tell *you* what we're going to do. We suck it up, at least for a little while. We pretend nothing happened. We don't even know each other." I can recognize the frenzy of my words as they spill from my mouth. "Then I'll make an excuse to leave. You and my mom can fulfill the promises you made Grandma Junie, and that's it. No one will ever have to know."

"Of course no one's going to know." He pinches the bridge of his nose. "This is why I don't fuck younger girls. Thinking with my stupid cock," he muses to himself.

"Yeah, 'cause it's your cock's fault," I snark.

He lifts his heated gaze to me. "You're right. It's yours. I thought you weren't getting in until today."

My cheeks heat at being caught in the lie but I square my shoulders. "So, you're used to just taking random women to your truck then?"

"Don't flatter yourself, girl," he punctuates, reminding me of the age difference between us. "It's none of your business, but I didn't think I'd have to worry about tongue-fucking my niece, as you so eloquently put it, when you weren't even supposed to be in town."

I swallow. This is unbelievable. *He's* unbelievable. "So mature to throw my words back in my face. I don't have to explain myself to you either." I plan to leave it at that but my brain just won't stop. The same words keep scrolling through my head on a never-ending loop of dread. "Oh my God, you're my uncle."

"I'm not your uncle," he grinds out. "We're barely related. By marriage," he tacks on. "Grow up."

My gaze snaps to his again. "You know what? I'll just tell my parents I had to go." I flail my hands around as if I can pick an excuse out of the ether. "I missed an exam or something. That's it. I missed an exam, and I have to go back to campus to take it. Perfect."

He practically snorts. "From what I hear, that's a terrible excuse. Your parents wouldn't believe it."

He's right. There's no way in this world or the next that I would miss an exam, but how the hell does he know that?

"You know, it's not my fault," he says, lips thinning. "The last picture I have of you, you were in pigtails."

I take a few calming breaths and lean against the wall next to him. "Yeah, that makes things better."

"I'm just saying, I wouldn't have recognized you."

"Obviously, that goes both ways," I mutter, trying to keep the edge out of my voice. "I've never even met you before. I'm not even sure I've even seen a picture..."

A man in a business suit walks by, and he does a double-take before coming to a stop in front of us. His black luggage that matches the rest of his attire comes to a rest next to him. "You're Cameron Michaels, right?"

My uncle sends me a pointed glare then turns back to the man. "Yeah, that's me."

My mouth practically drops open.

"Man, you were so good.."

Oh. *Ohhh...* This is about his previous football career.

Next to me, Cameron's face falls. His next words are a little less jovial. "Thanks. I appreciate it."

The stranger suddenly looks embarrassed. He grabs his luggage again and starts to walk away while he says, "Well, have a great Christmas."

Yeah, a great Christmas... It's starting out swell.

"You too, man," my uncle answers.

When he leans back against the wall, I can feel accusing eyes on me. My muscles turn to knots. I know he wants to say something about random people recognizing him but that I didn't. "Yeah, like I care about football, okay?" I explain. I'm sure I could've looked him up, but I didn't care to. He was no one my family actually wanted to know until Grandma died.

My phone rings, and I stare down at the screen to see my mom's picture there. I glance up briefly to see that her stupid stepbrother actually looks a little nervous.

With a deep breath, I answer, putting the phone to my ear. "Hey, Mom."

"Oh, honey," she says, voice distraught. "Bad news. Our flight got cancelled."

My gaze locks with my unfortunate companion.

Could this get any worse?

five

. . .

MOM PROMISED to get the first flight out she can. She was so frantic, I couldn't even tell her that we should just call the whole thing off. Maybe all of this is fate. We should disregard Grandma Junie's wishes and go about our lives without this guy in them.

But it means so much to her. Hearing the desperation in my mom's voice only made me feel selfish as I was trying to figure out excuses why I should leave. Here she is, trying desperately to get to us, and the only thing I can think of is getting away.

Maybe Uncle Cameron was right. We'll just pretend nothing happened. Which would be a little easier if the man was nicer. He's just a grumpy old asshole…with a skillful tongue. That's it.

When I told him my parents weren't coming, his face hardened so quick I thought it would crack down the middle where a huge vein popped out of his forehead.

I look away, taking a few deep breaths because I can barely look at his face without thinking about that *thing* that I'm determined not to think about.

"I guess it's just us," I trudge on. "I can get another place to stay."

He shakes his head, his jaw hard. "They'll probably get a flight out tomorrow, then they'll wonder why you aren't staying with me. Just come back to the inn," he demands, even though it sounds like the last thing he wants.

I rub a hand down my face. This is so not the way I pictured this initial meeting. I knew it would be awkward but I also imagined my uncle older, possibly with a beer belly, and of course, way less hot.

Without another word, he takes my luggage and starts to wheel it toward the automatic exit doors. I follow after, trying not to look at him the way I did last night. Large shoulders. Tapered waste. He has no business being an uncle to someone my age, that's for sure.

And that hat. That fucking hat. It gives him such a boyish charm that still wraps me up tight. The way he'd grinned and winked at me last night. We had a connection, for sure. I just didn't know it was wrong. So, so wrong.

He takes me right to his truck that's parked in an open lot. My gaze immediately goes to the back door. I want to tell him I can't get in this thing, but I can already predict his response. Something about telling me to grow up, I'm sure. So, I suck it up, watch as he throws my luggage in the truck bed, and then heaves himself into the front seat.

I stare at him discreetly for a little while. His face is pinched, obviously bothered by the circumstances, but all the little tidbits about his life that I know are coming back to me too. My grandma and his dad had a whirlwind romance that left my grandfather behind. Mom couldn't ever forgive her, and for the longest time, they didn't have a relationship. Grandma Junie was living it up at her new man's inn outside of Portland, Maine with a stepson who was an NFL star, and we were just living our lowly lives in Richmond while my mother self-destructed with alcohol until she came to the conclusion that she didn't even have to like her mother but she did have to like herself.

Grandma used to send picturesque postcards and pictures of the inn, letters and notes. If I saw them at all, it was because I dug them out of the trash. It always looked magical, and I was a jealous of her, and mad at my mom that we couldn't visit this place that looked like one of those Christmas inns from Hallmark movies.

At least I have that to look forward to.

I heave myself into the truck. The engine kicks to life, and heat starts pouring out of the vents. "So, I hear you took over the inn after your Dad died and um…" I stop my sentence. He didn't much like it when the stranger alluded to his career-ending injury, so I'm not bringing that up again.

"I did," he says, voice sharp.

"Do you like it?"

"It's a job."

I roll my eyes. So, I take that as a no? Or as a cue for me to stop talking? I was never very good at socializing, that's for sure.

While he stews next to me, driving the beast of a vehicle through the snow-covered streets expertly, I stare out the window. Eventually, the cityscape fades to a highway. When my uncle turns off the exit, I start to perk up. Eventually, I see the city sign. I recognize it in one of the pictures Grandma Junie sent. Winterhaven. The inches of snow clinging to the sign only makes it a more perfect scene, like the town is living up to its name.

As he drives down the narrow streets, I light up at all of the Christmas decor. Not one business isn't covered in green garland and red bows. Everything matches perfectly, and it looks like everyone inside each building should be wearing aprons and baking Christmas cookies and caroling to their heart's content. "Wow," I say in wonder. "It's exactly like Grandma said."

"June wrote to you about Winterhaven?"

"Well, yeah. Kind of," I say, peering over at him. His gaze is fixed on the road, but deep lines have set into his forehead. "Not a lot, actually. Well, I think she sent tons of things, but I didn't read them all," I say, nervous to admit. It was really bad at our house for a while, and it's all directly related to this man's father. I don't know how to navigate this part of our history coupled with the more recent, more *tragic* one as well.

"She loved it here," he says fondly, and I just get the briefest glimpse of the man from the pub last night. Charming and handsome. Happy, even.

The aromas of the truck smell the same too.

The way he took charge…

The dirty things that came out of his mouth. *Give it to me. It's all mine.*

The memories won't stop coming now. I squirm in my seat.

I'm relieved when he turns into a driveway. The inn comes into view, and I gasp. Not in sheer delight. In shock.

The inn looks nothing like Winterhaven. It doesn't even look anything like the pictures Grandma June used to send.

There are no Christmas decorations to be seen. The paint is peeling. The only thing seasonal about the building is the snow clinging to the ground and gathering on windowsills.

Before I can ask him what the fuck happened to the place, a woman comes running out of the front door, hands waving.

"Mr. Michaels, Mr. Michaels."

My uncle jumps out of the car, and I try not to eavesdrop as I hear her tell him that her husband has fallen in the snow and broken his leg, and she has to leave immediately.

He assures her with soft words, then sees her off with a smile as a plain-looking sedan pulls into the driveway and whisks her off as fast as the icy roads can take her.

I just sit there in the truck, not sure what to do. He spins, and I can tell already that he's morphed back into the grumpy asshole from the airport. "Fucking wonderful," he murmurs.

"What is it?"

He slams his door before reaching into the truck bed for my luggage and yanking it out. "She's my last remaining employee!" he barks, then trudges through the snow to what should be a walkway, but it's not shoveled. He throws the front door open and then does a double take when he realizes I'm not right next to him. "Are you coming or not?" he yells, glaring into the truck.

I breathe in deep, willing it out slowly. This fucking man… I guess everyone gets the nice guy routine unless you're me.

No wonder why he doesn't have any help.

Should I start counting down the hours now? Or wait?

six

. . .

SNOW FALLS OUTSIDE. I tap the glass of my bedroom window that faces toward the front drive, watching each unique flake flutter through the air and land below in a glistening kaleidoscope. It's all so beautiful.

The inn on the other hand is...like nice *adjacent*. It looks like it should be nice. It has all the cozy aspects. The patchwork quilt, the moody paint and dark wood trim. But it's not quite there. A must smell permeates from somewhere inside the dank room. The bed creaks. And the draft coming in from the window is chilly. Every time the wind blows outside, a phantom burst of air wraps around my body. I tap the glass again, and the windowpane rattles a little.

The love affair I had with this inn through pictures is slowly fading to reality.

And its owner is much like my mother feared all those years ago. He's a jock. Worse than that, he's a jock who can't jock anymore, so he's a grumpy asshole, not *only* an asshole.

I let out a breath, and the window in front of me fogs. I've procrastinated long enough. Grabbing my phone, I start downstairs for the first time since I got in yesterday. I can't spend the whole holiday avoiding my sexy as fuck uncle. After having all these hours alone to think about it, I've come to the conclusion that what we did was an honest mistake. Now that we know we're quasi related, I'm sure we'll be able to get along fine. All familial-like. One big fucked-up family like everyone else.

Still, I sneak down the steps, worried about seeing him again. My stomach twists as my foot hits the main floor. Then I freeze as a loud clatter erupts out of nowhere. Peeking my head into the closest room, I find an older couple seated at a small, circular table. They greet me with worried glances of their own. The woman's gaze darts toward a door on the far side, and I stare at it as a frustrated grunt sounds from just beyond it.

This must be the dining room…and beyond that, the kitchen.

"I should go help him," the woman says.

She's about to get up from the table when I head that way. "Do you guys need coffee? Juice?" I ask, instincts taking over. I may not care about this inn or this man, but my Grandma Junie sure did.

"Everything," the man mutters. "We need everything."

I turn, my lips thinning. Pushing open a swinging door, I stop in my tracks. Cameron Michaels is standing in the middle of the kitchen with his hands on his hips, staring down at…something splattered across the black and white checkered floor.

But that's not all of it. Dirty dishes are everywhere. Flour is strewn over the island like traces of snow. And smoke pours out of the oven in gray, billowy clouds. To top it all off, the smoke alarm starts beeping like an angry bystander.

"Shit!" Cameron springs into action, grabbing a dishtowel from the island and flapping it at the smoke alarm while I run to the oven to turn it off. Then, I sprint to the window above the sink and open it to let in some fresh air. When I turn, my uncle is scowling at me. "What are you doing? You're not supposed to be in here."

"What am *I* doing?" I counter. "You're burning the house down."

"I have it under control."

"Yeah, totally seems like you do."

Luckily, the blast of cold air and Cameron's incessant flapping helps the smoke alarm situation. It shuts off abruptly, and Cameron's hands drop to his side, dejected. Whatever is in the oven is unsavable. That's for sure.

"Listen," I tell him, a plan already forming in my mind. I like puzzles and problems, but I like fixing them even more. "You head out there with drinks. I'll figure something out in here."

He gazes at me suspiciously.

I sigh. Are we really going to do this? "This is the part where you yell at me. Yadda yadda, big ol' mean grumpy man routine, but then you realize that what I'm offering you is actually helpful, so please, let's skip the macho asshole bit and get to the part where we actually feed your guests. I assume that's what you're trying to do."

He still looks unsure, not moving from his spot. The poor dish towel dragging on the ground like he's Linus from Peanuts. Dear Lord, could this get any sadder?

"Trust me, I can't do anything worse than what you've already done," I assure him. I'm no chef, that's for sure, but I can certainly make breakfast. I point toward the door. "Juice. Coffee. Now."

"Fine," he gives in, though his voice is still sour. When he passes me, I notice the cutest smear of what looks like pancake batter across his shirt. Flour dots his forehead and is peppered throughout his hair. Smirking, I watch as he grabs a tray with coffee and juice already on it before bumping the swinging door with his backside and leaving me in peace.

Yep, totally not telling him he has ingredients all over him. He deserves it.

I get to work. I find a carton of eggs on the counter but have to wash a frying pan in order to scramble some. After getting them going, I search out a loaf of bread in the pantry. Eggs and toast might not be much, but at least it'll get something in his guests' stomachs.

Cameron comes back in with the tray. I peek behind

me to see that the cups full of coffee are still there. He dumps them out in the sink and then starts a new pot. He dribbles his fingers over the counter, his foot tapping in one of the few bare spots of the floor. I try not to laugh but that must catch his attention too. "What?" he snaps, eyeing me.

"Problem?" I ask, arching an eyebrow and looking at the coffee machine pointedly.

"Coffee was cold."

"That tends to happen when it just sits there," I say, amused.

"I don't find any of this funny," he grouses. "No receptionist. No cook."

Turning, I scramble the eggs. "Did they quit because of your winning personality?"

He marches toward me, and I turn my back to the stove at the sound of his heavy footsteps approaching. Holding the spatula in my hand between us like a shield, I glare daggers at him.

Stopping, he looks me up and down. "You of all people should know I can actually be quite nice. Especially when you were yelling, *Please. Yes, please.*"

A gasp rips from my throat. The heavy tone of orgasm-ridden female that pours from his mouth makes my face heat. Biting my lower lip, I peer up at the indent in the center of his bottom lip. "We said we weren't going to talk about that."

While I wait for him to answer, I notice the scruff is back on his face. He's no longer the clean-shaven man from the day before. I swear I'm still chafed from the beard burn he left on me, and that's all it takes for my thighs to ache at the memory of him there, eating me like I was a delicious meal.

He must not have the same fond memories because he glowers at me. "Consider me bringing it up as retaliation for not telling me I had flour in my hair…and on my forehead."

I peer up, and sure enough, the white specks are gone.

"Mrs. Williams told me."

His voice is menacing. Almost dangerous. The toast pops behind me, and I jump. As if sensing his prey is ready to be taken, he moves in close, pressing me against the stove. "I suggest you watch that attitude before I turn you over my knee."

My mouth suddenly goes dry. He turns away at the telltale sound of the coffeemaker finishing its brewing. The delicious aroma of good coffee fills the air. It takes me a moment to gather my bearings, and he's already halfway out the door when I find my voice. "You know I don't have to help you."

"You also don't have to be a brat about helping me either."

He disappears, and I turn, slamming my fist down. I can't believe—

My skin sizzles, and a fiery pain shoots up my hand.

"Fuck," I hiss. I snatch my hand away from the stove top where it had gotten too close to a burner.

Seriously?

seven

. . .

WHEN CAMERON WALKS BACK IN, I have a drenched paper towel wrapped around my palm and I'm stubbing my toe into the floor over and over in hopes that will deflect from the searing pain in my hand.

As soon as I hear him, I march back to the traitorous stove to check on the eggs. I continue to scramble them, still holding the wet towel to my skin before turning the burner off.

"What's that?" my uncle asks, peering over.

I square my shoulders. "Nothing." My words come out clipped. If he hadn't distracted me earlier, I wouldn't be in this predicament.

"It doesn't look like nothing."

"Just a minor...burn," I tell him, moving to search for some butter in the refrigerator.

He sighs, the sound so full off annoyance that it

straightens my spine in an instant. I slam the fridge door and start to walk back to the toaster.

"Come here," he demands.

"I'm fine."

He rattles away in the cupboards as I place the dish full of single-serve butters on the counter next to the toaster. "I said come here," he grunts. When I don't listen, he grabs the crook of my elbow and firmly steers me toward the island. Once I'm there, he pours milk into a shallow bowl then points to one of the stools. "Sit."

I do as he asks, eyeing him warily. He takes my burnt hand in his with a gentleness I didn't know he possessed. "Careful," I tell him, grimacing as he unwraps the now room temperature paper towel.

He continues as if I didn't say anything, but his touch is careful. "Water doesn't help burns," he tells me, using his voice for *other* people. Not the one he usually uses for me. He gently lays my hand into the bowl of milk. "This should take care of it."

"Milk?"

He shrugs. "No idea. I only know that it works."

Staying where he is for a few moments, he peers from me to my hand. He takes the hat off his head, blowing out an exasperated breath. "I should… I'm going to serve the food now," he says finally.

I nod as he grabs a clean serving bowl from a cupboard to the right of the stove even though it's entirely too big. He scrapes the eggs into it and then places the eggs and toast on a tray to walk out into the dining room.

A sense of relief washes over me as soon as he's gone. The milk is already making my palm feel better but also, the guests have at least something to eat. Sure, the kitchen looks like a tornado went through it, but that can be cleaned up.

What really has my attention, though, is Cameron Michaels. How can one person have so many personalities?

The door swings back open, and the man in question makes another appearance. "They look much more agreeable now than when I first went out there," he announces.

"People tend to get happier when they know there's food involved."

He sets the tray down, sitting on the stool opposite me. "Sorry about your hand." A few more seconds go by, when he continues, "I'm trying to find someone to come in and work, but it's that time of year when everyone wants to be at home with their families, so I don't have any takers."

"It is pretty close to Christmas," I agree.

He scowls as if he didn't need the reminder.

"Listen, I'll help," I offer. "I don't have anything to do until my parents get here anyway, and it seems like you could use it."

He lifts a brow. "I could, huh?" he asks, his voice taking on that asshole edge I've become accustomed to.

"You live in the Christmas Capital of the North, and

you don't even have any decorations up," I use as evidence to support my statement. "No tree in the living room. No lights outside. I can't imagine why the only two guests you have are Prissy Pants One and Two, and I bet they're contemplating leaving."

He shakes his head, a humorless laugh escaping his throat. "Been here less than twenty-four hours, and you already think you know what's going on."

"I don't think. I know," I counter. "When was the last time the inn was painted? Or hell, a smidge of preventative maintenance completed. There's a draft coming in through my window, and—"

"Oh, a draft," he says, standing from his stool so hard that it nearly topples over. "Do you want to put in a complaint form, Princess?"

"Is there one?" I ask. "Because if there is, I'd like to talk to someone who gives a fuck."

He steps in next to me, towering over my seated form until I can see that the stubble on his chin leads almost all the way down to his Adam's apple. "I liked it better when your mouth was preoccupied."

The infuriating look he gives me makes my whole body heat. "For someone who wanted to act like nothing happened, you seem preoccupied with it."

"Maybe because I liked you better when you were riding my face...*not* talking or jumping to conclusions."

My nipples peak. Forget about my hurt palm, I'm thrust right back into the way he'd ensnared me with his web two days ago. But this time, he isn't seducing me with his good looks and bold behavior, it's with a match of words. "Thinking about your niece that way… How naughty," I muse. I can barely breathe. I know I'm playing with fire here, but I can't stop.

His eyes spark. "You're not my niece."

"Would Grandma Junie say that?"

He smirks, leaning over me again until he turns his hat around and glares down. "You think you're a big girl, but you aren't. You're trying to play a game with me that you'll lose." He leans over, rasping into my ear, "You came so fast and hard on my tongue that I'm not so sure you've even been fucked before. You might as well put your hair up in pigtails again."

His hot breath has me squirming, but it's that stupid backwards hat that has me not wanting to put an end to this. It's too sexy. I press my thighs together to relieve the ache. I'm definitely not a virgin, but he's not exactly wrong. It had been too long since I'd been touched like that. "Why do I get the feeling that you would enjoy that too much?" I spread my knees wide, moving my knee around his so that he can step into me as I move my ass to the edge of the stool.

His thigh brushes my apex, and I start to move against his corded muscles. My sweater dress has ridden up high across my stomach, so there's only the barest of barriers between the two of us—my thin leggings and even thinner panties—and I just happen to be soaked through both.

"Are you wet for me, Baby Girl?" he growls.

Oh, dear God, there's that praising mouth of his.

"Uh huh," I murmur, grabbing the back of his thigh and bringing myself closer.

"Check."

Um, excuse me. "What?"

"I want to see your hands dip into that perfect pussy."

It's that mouth of his that has my hand sneaking between us before I'm even conscious of the fact. But then I stop abruptly when my burn flares in pain. "Fuck," I pant, switching to my left. I've never done this with my uncoordinated hand, but there's a first time for everything.

Working my way under my leggings, I settle over my panties. Just as I thought, they're damp with my pleasure and soaking even more. I move the lacy material to the side and slide my fingers through my folds, albeit a little clumsily.

"Tell me," he urges, his eyes hooded, the green flecks there sparking dangerously.

"I'm wet," I pant. "For you."

"For me?"

"Yes, Uncle." I don't even know why the words spill out. They're so wrong, so filthy, but I can't help the way my body responds to them.

"Let me taste."

I work two fingers into my pussy, pumping inside myself as my mouth drops open in ecstasy before pulling them out, holding the tips to his lips.

He eyes me before moving forward, licking with the tip of his tongue before wrapping his whole mouth around my fingers, taking them in to the knuckle. His eyes close with a moan. Flicking his tongue out, he runs it all over my fingers until he pulls away. "Like sin," he murmurs.

Lowering my hand again, I go back to my task. I'm disjointed this way, stroking myself with my useless hand, but my body keeps wanting more and more. I growl in frustration until he places his hand over mine above my leggings. "Let me see you fuck yourself." He urges me forward, making my strokes more fluid.

"Yes, Uncle," I breathe.

"Fuck. Why is that so hot?"

His palm rubs my clit as he forces my fingers into my pussy over and over again. My harsh breaths fill the kitchen.

"Tell your uncle how fucking good it feels."

"Oh God," I moan. "I want more."

"Is your pussy starving for me?"

"Yes," I grind out.

He picks up the pace, driving my fingers into me until I'm just lifting my hips to take it.

"Say, Uncle Cam. Say it. When you come, I want my name on your lips."

"Oh, fuck me," I breathe. Part of me wants to stop this in favor of his cock pistoning in and out of me, but I don't want this to end either.

He reaches out, finding my nipple through my sweater and teasing it. He brushes and strokes, giving it a little pinch until my orgasm builds and builds.

"Oh God, it's coming."

"You mean, Uncle Cam, it's coming."

I let out a moan as he drives me higher and higher.

A knock sounds on the kitchen door, and I panic, turning my head toward the swinging door.

"I'm not stopping, Baby Girl, so you may as well just take it."

I squirm, my body ratcheting higher and higher.

"Uncle Cam," I breathe, my body almost cresting. I'm still staring at the kitchen door in alarm. They could come in. Anyone could. And what would they find? The owner of the inn helping his niece finger fuck herself?

"You're fucking gorgeous like this," he breathes.

I lock gazes with him, and it's then that I explode. "Uncle Cam!" I scream out as my body squeezes around my fingers. My body keeps spasming and spasming. I start to cry out again as he presses my head into his chest, stifling my cries.

"Everything's fine," he throws out over his shoulder, his deep voice rumbling in his chest.

"Oh my God. Oh my God," I pant as I ride out my pleasure. When I'm spent, I just sit there, my body relaxing incrementally, tension oozing out of me.

He nips at my earlobe. "You're right. I would love the fuck out of those pigtails. Just as long as you keep that pretty little mouth shut."

eight

. . .

THE KITCHEN IS FINALLY CLEAN. I've got the local radio station playing me Christmas tunes, sweat dripping down my back, and glaring out at Cameron Michaels as he chops firewood.

Just as long as you keep that pretty little mouth shut.

Well, that's a surefire way to get me to do the opposite. God, I've never been so mad at myself in my entire life. One guy—fucking related to me—who knows how to work my body, and I give up my freaking feminist card. No. Absolutely freaking not. Consider it laminated and stamped because no more. Uncle Cam can kiss my ass.

I'm taking back control, and since it's my holiday, too—stuck here alone with him—I'm going to make the best of it.

With several deep breaths, I close my eyes, truly listening to the song blaring out of the radio. *Deck the halls with boughs of holly. Fa la la la la la la la la.*

True that. I'm about to deck some mothereffing halls, whether *Uncle Cam* likes it or not.

As soon as I figure out where the decorations are, of course. They're probably stuck right up his prickly ass.

Well, that isn't true to the Christmas spirit. … They're probably stuck right up his holly holder.

How about that?

Smiling to myself, I grab my jacket and head out to the backyard. The bite in the air nearly takes my breath away as I step outside. My breath clouds in front of me. There's a fresh couple of inches of snow on the ground, and before I even get to the haphazardly thrown firewood, my boots are soaked through.

Despite the fact that it's freezing out here, Uncle Cam is sweating. He wipes his brow before bringing the axe down on a piece of wood, splitting it in two with a loud thwack. He kicks one of the sides off the stump and places another that needs to be cut on top. I watch him do it again, the pure concentration on his face as he brings the axe down reminding me of the look on his face earlier. He's ditched his ballcap for a beanie that still looks sexy as fuck, even though I'm not looking at him in that way anymore.

Eventually, he gazes up. "Are you just going to stand there ogling?"

He fucking wishes.

Before I can tell him what I'm doing out there, he motions toward the firewood. "Why don't you take some inside and set it next to the fireplace in the dining room."

I lift a brow. I said I'd help him, not be at his beck and call. Regardless, I take a deep breath and conjure up some Christmas spirit. My mother would say that the meanest of all need more than the others, but I still don't know what Cameron Michaels' problem is. Squatting, I pick some wood up, glancing up at him as I do. "I'll help if you tell me where the Christmas decorations are."

"How should I know?" he asks, bringing down the axe again. The loud thwack makes my stomach squeeze.

If he's trying to freak me out, it won't work. "Oh, I don't know. Maybe because you own the place."

He shrugs, getting another piece ready. "Try the attic."

He steps back, heaving the axe over his shoulder before bringing it back down harder than the last time. I stand. "You really don't care about Christmas, do you?"

"Not really," he mutters. "Why should I?"

"Oh, I don't know. Because it's literally a time for caring. To spend time with family and—"

"Well, I'm short on family, so…"

It's like everything this man says is to drive people away. "Suit yourself," I counter. I wish Grandma Junie had mentioned that this guy had the personality of a gnat. That would've gone a long way in deciding whether to fulfill her wish or not. I'm so close to calling my mom and telling her and Dad not to bother coming, but they're probably on their way. I haven't been able to get a hold of them all morning, so fingers crossed they're in the air, flying to rescue me from this hellhole. If worse comes to worst, we can find another inn to spend Christmas together.

Turning, my mind already on digging out decorations , I freeze when I feel two pats on my butt. "Good girl," Uncle Cam breathes.

Good girl? Good...*girl?*

I ignore the way my body heats at his praise, and instead, I drop the firewood right where I'm standing and march back into the house. He can *good girl* somewhere else because this girl is trying to keep her dignity intact.

Right before I heave open the front door, I look over my shoulder to find him leaning on the handle of his axe, a full grin on display.

It only makes me even more mad as I stomp into the house.

nine

. . .

THE ATTIC DOOR sticks as I yank it open. It's only the third door I tried on the second floor, and the only one that proved not to be a closet. *Yass,* I congratulate myself internally. *I'm coming for you Christmas decorations.*

The stairs creak under my weight. I hug my arms to myself. If I thought the draft was bad in my room, this stairwell to the attic isn't heated at all. I turn, going back down to the attic door to close it so I don't freeze Cameron Michaels' remaining tenants right out of the inn.

I blow into my hands, rubbing then together before they turn to ice. Hopefully, this is a quick job. If my Grandma Junie is as organized as my mom, there'll just be a tub labeled *X-MAS decorations* that I'll be able to grab and carry downstairs.

The top of the staircase opens up to two pitched

areas. I can walk without stooping through the middle, but the gables sloping down are only good for storage. And they've definitely used every nook and cranny. There's an old TV set. Several dressers. A couple of standing mirrors that freak me out. And amidst those other things, there are boxes and boxes…and even more boxes. In fact, there are so many boxes that the only clear space in the attic is the walkway down the center that leads to a circle window that overlooks the side yard.

Part of me just wants to turn around, but the other part of me refuses to be bogged down by all the stuff. It'll be nice to have the decorations up before my mom and dad get here. Of course, there are the other guests too. I don't care what they think about my uncle, but it would be nice for them to get some Christmas cheer, I'm sure.

The first few boxes I look through just have old clothes in them, musty sheets, and a bunch of knick-knacks. In between every box, I stop to rub my arms, trying to bring some warmth back into them.

Okay, if I were Christmas decorations, where would I be?

I spy a couple of boxes to themselves on the other side of the attic and decide to check those next. I see a distinct C on one and joy fills me until I get the box open. Inside are a bunch of trophies. I pull one out, turning it around to find that it's for football. They're *all* for football. There must be at least a dozen in here, and all of them are inscribed with my uncle's name. High-

School All-American. College All-American. MVP. Most Running Yards.

Wow. I guess he was something special.

The next box with a big C is filled with old jerseys. There are small maroon and yellow ones that look aged. Then there are bigger gray ones, and in the very bottom, I find a New England Captains Jersey. Michaels, number twenty-nine. I don't know why but I bring it to my face, breathing the jersey in, but all I smell is must and dankness.

I'm tempted to Google his name, to figure out what happened. I've been trying to honor his privacy, but fuck it, I can't take it any longer. Reaching into my back pocket, I come up empty. Ugh. I must've left my cell phone downstairs somewhere. I'll just have to search for it later.

All this history though. You don't keep something like this unless you don't want to give it away. But to not have it displayed somewhere, I'm willing to bet there's some hurt that goes with all of this stuff too.

His words from earlier ring through my head. *Well, I'm short on family.*

Uneasiness churns my stomach. Maybe he's just lonely. Or lost. If Grandma Junie was the only person he had left, I can imagine what her death did to him.

I rub my temples, blowing out a breath, before boxing all of his gear back up. It feels icky to look through his stuff.

Pushing those boxes aside, I keep combing through more until I spy a very small pine tree in the corner.

"Ah!" I cry out, pushing boxes aside before I pick up the small tree. It has two small, crisscrossed pieces of wood for its base and the tiniest of ornaments hanging from its branches. If this is here...

Sure enough, the boxes surrounding the small tree are full of Christmas decorations. I'm up to ten of them as I leave them by the stairwell to take downstairs.

One of the boxes in the back is actually labeled Christmas. I run my hand over the swirly C, recognizing it. This is Grandma Junie's handwriting. Peering inside, I find a red sleigh being pulled by eight reindeer. The reindeer's antlers hold pictures in their grip, and in each one, there's a picture of a member of my family. At the front is a picture of me when I was a baby dressed in a frilly red dress. There are more as I grow up, but they stop when I'm about twelve. Then after that, there are some of Mom and my dad, then of my mom alone when she was a baby.

I run my fingers over it. Grandma Junie had this the whole time. Even when my mom wouldn't talk to her. Even when she ignored her, she still had us here.

My heart breaks a little. My eyes heat, but I force back the tears and add the box with the others. I'm going to be pretty busy putting up all of this stuff. And, I haven't even started dinner yet.

Maybe I can get Uncle Cam to get off his prickly ass to come help bring this stuff down.

I pick up the small pine tree that helped me discover the rest and trudge down the steep stairs with it. I get to the bottom and turn the door handle...nothing.

The door won't open.

I keep turning and turning, pushing as hard as I can, but it won't budge.

I'm locked in the attic.

The *freezing cold* attic.

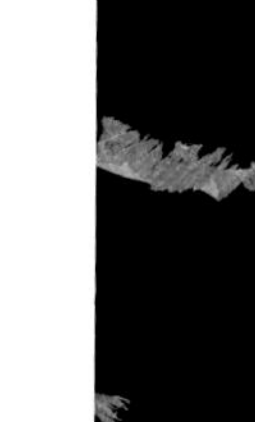

ten

. . .

EVERY DANK, musty piece of fabric I could find in the attic—old clothing, pillowcases, drapes, you name it—is currently wrapped around me, keeping me from freezing my ass off. Still, I'm not close to being considered comfortable. I've been sneezing my ass off from all the dust, my nose is cold and running, and after I banged on the door for more than half an hour to no avail, I had to think of a different plan.

Since then, I've been parked at the bottom of the staircase, ears straining. I've shouted. I've cried. I've panicked. I don't like the feeling of being stuck here. Imaginary spiders crawl all over me, and to make matters worse, the sun has gone down, and with that, the light in the attic has slowly faded. Shadows are everywhere. Creeping. I've searched and searched for a light switch or just plain lights anywhere, but there's nothing.

It's been hours, and I'm still trapped. Every few

minutes, I bang on the door, then wrap myself up as tight as can be. A few times, I've almost fallen asleep, but the fear of having to spend the night in this place keeps me from doing so. I want my drafty bedroom. At least there's a humongous quilt that's toasty warm along with *some* heat. My fingers and toes have gone numb. What little warmth there was in the attic has all been sucked out as day turned to evening. I can barely see an inch in front of my face now.

But there are noises.

Little skittering noises. Thumps that sound like footsteps.

Or I could be losing my mind.

I bang on the door again. "Help!!!" It's only the umpteenth time I've done it. How in the world is he not looking for me right now? He knew what I was going to do. I told him about decorating. Then again, I hid in my room all night yesterday.

Fuck. Fuck. Fuck.

Tears spring to my eyes again as I lay my head on my arm. I haven't felt my butt in an hour due to the uncomfortable stairs. My back hurts from being balled up tight. I just want out. Why is being here such a nightmare? I expected it to be bad, but this is so much worse.

"Jingle bells, jingle bells. Jingle all the way," I breathe. I might totally be losing it now, but singing is better than being in my head and wondering for the hundredth time if that feeling on the back of my neck is a huge ass spider waiting to bite me or just a ghost come to take me to Christmases past.

"Lilianne? Lilianne?"

I perk up, immediately standing to pound on the door. I almost trip, landing with my hands outstretched against the wood. "Here. I'm here. Help!" I call out. The burn on my palm aches as I slam it against the door.

The door in front of me creaks. It almost bows as someone tugs on the knob.

"I'm locked in," I call out.

He yanks a few more times, and the door finally gives. I fall out after it, landing directly in my uncle's arms. "Jesus, girl." Slumping against him, I close my eyes at his warm embrace. He feels like a boiling pot of water compared to my shivering body. "You're as cold as an icicle."

"Because I've been st-stuck in the stupid attic for hours!"

He picks me up, cradling me to his chest as he takes me to a room on the far side of the house. He sets me down on a counter in between two sinks. Spinning, he turns to twist the faucet on to a huge garden tub. The water comes rushing out, sounding like a waterfall to my noise-deprived ears.

He comes right back over, taking my hands in his and rubbing them between his own. I hiss as he hits my burn. "Sorry. I forgot. I was actually trying to find you to see if you needed anything for it."

My skin pricks as he works heat into the chilled

layers. Little by little, the numbness goes out of my legs, but in its place, needles prick all over.

I groan at how uncomfortable it is. Uncle Cam looks on with a concerned gaze. "I should've realized you were gone sooner."

I shake my head. Despite cursing him up and down while I was up there, there really was no way for him to know.

He checks the water temperature and then drops the plug in the tub.

"This will get you nice and warm," he says as the tub starts to fill. He comes over to unwrap all the extra layers from me. "You must've been freezing."

"J-just a little," I stutter, teeth still clacking together.

When he gets to my actual clothes, he doesn't stop. He yanks at the bottom of my sweater dress, pulling it over my head and dropping it to the floor. I cover myself up, crossing my hands over my bra.

He gives me a pointed look. "Not the time to act modest when I've had my hands all over those tits, Baby Girl."

I swallow, his words doing more to warm me up than any of the layers I'd held around me.

He pulls me off the counter, steadying me on my feet. My leggings are next, and I'm too numb to realize he's taken my panties with them until I see them on the ground.

"Jeez," I say, placing a hand over my bare mound.

"And we both know I've been there, too." The smirk and wink he gives me reminds me of the guy from the first night. But we both know he'll be smacking my ass and telling me not to talk soon, so I keep my distance anyway.

He reaches around to unhook my bra, but I wiggle out of his grip. "I can do it."

"Stop being a child," he scolds. "Let me help."

"I've got it," I tell him. I stand back, trying to work at the clasps, but my fingertips still have needles being pricked into them so I can't quite get it.

"Let me help," he says again, stepping forward.

I shimmy away from him, immediately getting in the water to keep my distance. The hot water scalds my feet, sending the needles even further in. "Ow, ow, ow."

But here Uncle Cam is again, coming toward me. I sit right down—my bra still on—and grimace as the hot water coats my skin all the way up to my neck.

"I've never met anyone as stubborn as you," he grinds out.

I shrug, not able to talk at first as the pinpricks keep making their way over my skin in waves of pain. "I guess you haven't met y-yourself."

"Don't move," he orders.

A piece of hard steel presses into my chest. I look down to find that he has a knife in his hand, hooked under the center of my bra. "What are you doing?" I exclaim.

True terror threads through me as I do exactly what he told me not to do. I start to thrash, water going everywhere.

eleven

. . .

HE GIVES a quick tug with the knife, and the two sides of my bra fall open, revealing my breasts.

Anger surges through me. "That was my bra!"

"And now it's not," he says, lips thinning.

Flicking his knife again, he cuts the straps in two until he can just tug my bra out of the water, leaving me bare-chested.

I hold my arms over my breasts. "What if I didn't want you to do that?"

"Oops," he mutters as he starts to unbutton his jeans. He lowers the zipper, spreading the sides of his pants apart, showing off the wide band of his boxers.

"What are you doing?" I gasp.

"Getting in with you."

He sheds his shirt next, stepping out of his jeans until he's in his boxers and hat. He casts his hat to the side, yanking down his briefs next.

"Body heat is what you need," he explains.

"I—I don't," I say, but the truth is, I'm already gawking at his cock. It's thick and veiny, and I'll be damned if he's not always erect like he's an eighteen-year-old addicted to porn. "Isn't that why you drew me a bath?"

"No, I drew you a bath as an excuse to get your beautiful ass naked."

He steps in, the water splashing around the sides. I try to move out of his way, but he's already between my legs, pinning my hips to the bottom of the tub. His thick cock slides up my belly.

He might be right. I'm certainly not thinking about how cold I am right now. I'm actually in awe at the douse of heat that just enveloped me.

"We shouldn't," I say, but my hand reaches out to grasp a handful of his ass anyway.

"No, we shouldn't," he says, his cock prodding my entrance.

I fall open for him. He grips the head of his cock in his hands, using it to rub my clit in torturous circles.

"How are you so fucking good at this?" I ask, moving against him. My breath is already coming out in unsteady pants.

"Uncle Cam."

"Huh?"

"It's 'How are you so fucking good at this, Uncle Cam?' Remember?"

He circles my entrance, and I press my knees into the sides of the tub. I'm practically salivating for him. "How about, fuck me, Uncle Cam?"

"My pleasure."

Despite his words, he doesn't give me what I ask for right away. Instead, he lowers on top of me, his hands searching out my breasts, playing with my sensitive nipples. "I thought you'd ran away from me again. That you planned to hide out in your room all night." He takes a mouthful of my breast, closing his eyes as he suctions onto it, teasing my peak with the tip of his tongue. He releases it, and my body immediately arches into him, searching out his mouth once more. "I was going to punish you."

"How so?" I ask, watching the way his dark stare eats me up. His stubble glides across my wet skin, the friction like sandpaper but oh so delicious.

He licks his lips. "It's more like punishing me," he says, voice breathy. He cups my breast, giving it a squeeze before trailing his fingers down my body to play with my folds. "Forbidden fruit."

"Is that why you want to fuck me, Uncle Cam? Because you shouldn't?"

He pivots against me, that glorious cock of his sliding up my belly again. "Because I hate myself," he grinds out. "And you should too. I'm double your age."

"What happened to the guy who said it was all about experience?"

"That guy thought he was talking to a no-named stranger."

He inserts one finger, working it into me in a slow, lip-biting rhythm.

"But you're not a stranger. You're June's granddaughter." He locks gazes with me. "So why do I want to fuck you so good right now?" He takes his finger out only to insert one more, circling and penetrating at the same time. "Why do I want you to call me Uncle Cam as you take my dick?"

I reach up, playing with my nipples as he finger fucks me. All this forbidden talk has me on edge. It's like an ignition to a spark. It's so, so wrong. But if it's so wrong, why does it feel so fucking good?

"We can go to therapy to talk about it, but later," I tell him. "Now, it's time to come up with fodder for us to talk about."

Reaching down, I cup his cock. I stroke it, feeling every ridge in my left palm. I've left my feminism at the door again, but I'm fine with that. I'll pick it back up when I leave this house. When I go back to school to all the hard work and the never-ending classes.

I angle toward him. A brief thought flits through my mind, *Am I really going to fuck this man?*

Yes, I am. Willingly. A fun romp. A secret only for us to know.

I pull his fingers out of me, but instead of feeling the head of his cock next, he flips me over. My knees hit the tub, water splashing all around as he lifts my hips, his cock sliding against me from behind. I grasp the side of the tub, looking up to find my own reflection in a mirror on the opposite wall.

Reaching around, he rubs my clit, and I can't help but ask, "What is this? Your porn studio?"

He actually grins. "The honeymoon suite."

Whatever snarky reply that popped into my head is immediately silenced when he grips my hips, pushing into me. My knuckles turn white as he goes all the way in, not holding anything back. My mouth falls open, and I catch his reaction in the mirror, too. Complete and utter pleasure. "Fuck. You're so tight." He moves just his hips, grinding into me in big circles. "I've been thinking about this pussy since McCallister's."

Length and girth must come with age too because fuck. He's almost more than I can take.

The fact that I was so cold just a few minutes ago feels like a distant memory because I'm firing on all cylinders now.

"Do other guys do you like this?" he pries, starting a slow, steady rhythm.

I shake my head. Not that he needs his ego-stroked, but no, I've never been fucked like this. He narrows his gaze, then tugs my hair with a pointed look. "No, Uncle Cam," I stutter out.

He pulls back on my hair and keeps going so that I stand on my knees. He keeps grinding into me, his free hand moving up my body, putting me into perfect position before covering my breasts with his rough palm. "Look at me fuck you. You're so beautiful like this. Taking my bare cock."

Jesus hell. I hadn't even… Thankfully, I'm on birth control because the thought hadn't even entered my mind. I'm usually the thinking type. The one to analyze everything, but he rips that from me whenever he's near.

"Eyes up," he demands, putting pressure on my scalp until I lock gazes with him again. He's stroking my nipple in time with his movements. Water sloshes around us but that's only secondary because I'm hyper fixated on him. On every ridge stroking in and out of my pussy.

His stubble rubs against my temple, and I reach up to wrap my hands around his face, holding him steady so that we just stare at one another.

"You shouldn't feel this fucking good," he moans.

"Neither should you."

His jaw hardens. He removes my hands from around him and then forces me back into all fours where he starts to fuck me hard and fast. The wet slaps of our bodies coming together fills my ears. My breasts jiggle in front of me as I hold onto the side of the tub, white knuckling it as all the pleasure pressurizes inside of me.

It's almost too much to take all at once. I barrel forward, but I'm scared too. All the emotion, every overwhelming pinpoint of pleasure. "You're okay," he says, as if he can read the scared look on my face. "I've got you."

"I'm—" I pant, unable to say it in words.

"I know. You're taking me so good, Baby Girl. So fucking good," he says, strained.

There's only one obvious place this is going, but the feeling is too consuming. "I—" I cry out, loud this time. I've never felt such a tornado of pleasure before. He's consuming me. That's what this is.

Reaching around, he places his hand over my mouth just as I scream out my orgasm. He only mutes the unintelligible sounds and moans pouring from me without thought or care. He just keeps driving me higher and higher until there's a hitch in his rhythm.

He stutters, then pulls out of me while I fall forward against the tub.

Holy shit.

I don't even recognize the girl staring back at me in the mirror. She's freshly fucked and smirking, still riding the high of aftershocks as I peer at the sexy-as-sin man behind me.

That's all this is. Just one big sin.

twelve

. . .

WHILE I SERVE dinner to the Williams' who seem in a much better mood than this morning, Cam brings down the Christmas decorations. I refuse to set foot in that third-story dungeon again. I chat with them for a little while, asking about their day around town. They hold hands over the table, and the whole scene makes everything seem so special. They're sitting closest to the fireplace, candles that I found burning between them, and I'm not trying to toot my own horn, but maybe I'm exceptionally good at this hospitality thing.

I pick at leftovers in the kitchen as Cam comes in, dusting his hands off. Pointing toward a full plate, I tell him to grab a seat. He does so, immediately eating. It's no wonder that he's starved, we certainly worked ourselves up an appetite earlier.

"I made a grocery list," I tell him. "You have enough food here for a few days for the number of guests expected, but we'll need some more soon. Plus, we still need everything for Christmas dinner."

He peers up at me, brows furrowed.

I shrug. "I looked through your reservation log. You know, you should probably go digital. Maybe even set up an online reservation system through your website. I know *I* hate talking to people on the phone. I bet your reservations would increase."

"What makes you think we have a website?" he asks, stuffing his face with a forkful of macaroni and cheese.

"Well, I'd start there then."

His fingers flex around the fork. I can feel the tension in the air thicken, but I'm really not in the mood to fight with him, so I try to head it off. "Of course, you can do whatever you want. It's your inn."

I put my dish in the sink, and then head out to tackle the Christmas decorations. First, I assess what's in each box and then put them into two stacks. One for outside decorations, and one for inside. Since this place could use some Christmas cheer, I start with the interior first.

Mr. and Mrs. Williams are still in the dining room, so I quickly run up to their room with a few things. The door isn't locked, which I'm not surprised about, so I put the small tree up on their mantle, and then a string of garland to frame out the fireplace. It's not much, but it's enough. When I turn, however, I notice their bed hasn't been made, so I quickly fluff up the pillows and make their bed, throwing the patchwork pillows on last. Then I go around, straightening the room, just like housekeeping staff does at the hotels I've stayed at in the past. With one last check, I call the room good before going back to my duty.

I start in the sitting room where the largest fireplace is. I frame it out with green garland, attaching little red bows every so often. Finding Santa statues and reindeer, I set those out first. Then, there's a sleeping Santa that when you turn it on, it snores to the tempo of Jingle Bells. While I work, I put holiday music on my Pandora station and go with it. By the time I'm finished, it looks like Christmas threw up in this room, and it's also almost eleven p.m.

The only thing missing is a Christmas tree. And since there wasn't one to be found in the attic, I'm guessing they get a real one. If I close my eyes, I can almost smell the pine scent of Christmases past.

The door nudges open, and I peer over my shoulder to find Cam in the mouth of the doorway. His gaze roams around the room. "Jesus."

"No, couldn't find one of those," I retort.

"There's that mouth again."

"It never stops," I tell him. "It's attached to my face."

I wait for another grumpy reaction, but one doesn't come. Finally, I search him out again and find him kneeling next to the windowsill where I placed the sleigh and reindeer with my family's pictures on it. "June loved this one."

"I see the pigtails," I tell him, motioning to the fourth picture back.

He smirks, shaking his head.

The room goes quiet except for the soft hum of Silent Night playing on my phone's speaker. "So, you and my grandma were close?" I hedge, not sure if he'll want to talk about this. I assumed that we'd all have a family discussion when my parents got here, but since I haven't heard from them all day, I don't know what's going on.

"I think so," he says, lips thinning. "She helped me a lot…afterward."

He doesn't specify but I know he's talking about his football career. "I found your old trophies in the attic." He whips his head toward me, so I talk quicker. "I couldn't find the decorations at first, so I opened up everything. You have one full of trophies and another full of old jerseys…"

He swallows, looking back at the picture-filled sleigh once more. "Those were the days," he says, and his voice is laced with so much pain that it almost physically hurts.

"So, since we both know I've never even looked you up, what exactly happened?" I ask. My heart pounds. I fully expect him to tell me off since it's really none of my business, but I also feel like if a guy puts his dick in you, you deserve a little bit of background information, you know?

He stands to his full height, then retreats to the couch on the far wall. "Just another sad story about a career that ended before it should. Well, before I was ready anyway. Not sure if anyone else cares."

I move closer to him. "Well, that doesn't sound like the truth. The guy at the airport recognized you."

He shrugs. He's almost entirely retreated into the couch now. "It doesn't seem like enough when at one point, my whole goal was to have the entire world chanting my name."

"I'm sorry that happened." My stomach squeezes, and I really don't know what else to say. "But you seem okay now. Maybe—"

He stops me before I go anywhere else with that sentence. "It's a spine injury, Lilianne. I can't risk it unless I want to gamble never being able to walk again."

I bite my lip. I wasn't expecting that answer. Shit.

"Most of the time it doesn't bother me, but sometimes it flares up, especially if I do something too physical."

My mind wanders back to him splitting wood and the unopened Christmas decorations in the attic. Maybe he just couldn't... Maybe he can't decorate the house either. Or the maintenance it needs.

Shit. I'm a terrible person.

I heave out a breath, ready to tell him I'm sorry when a call on my phone interrupts the Christmas music. Peering over, I see my mom's face, so I snatch the phone up with excitement. "Mom?"

I don't hear anything at first, then a sob comes through.

There are no flights out before Christmas. Not a single one.

Mom's too incoherent on the phone to talk, so I tell her I'll call her later after she's calmed down. I reassure her that I'm fine, but my eyes prick with unshed tears. "They can't get here before Christmas," I tell Cam, dropping the phone onto the coffee table.

He reaches for me, yanking me down into his lap until I'm straddling him. "Good."

I lift my brows. My first reaction is to tell him to fuck off, but the way he's staring at me makes me keep my mouth shut.

"Because I'm not done making you mine yet, and I don't want to sneak around my own house while I try to fuck you."

thirteen

. . .

BREAKFAST HAS BEEN SERVED. New guests checked in. Kitchen is cleaned and stocked, and it's two days before Christmas.

Merry Christmas Eve Eve.

Uncle Cam swats my ass playfully, then heads toward the swinging doors. "I don't know where you think you're going," I call out after him.

He turns, leering at me as if I've just given him an invitation to take me across the kitchen island.

I give him a solid stare in return. It's hard enough to function without him looking at me like that all the time. "You're taking me to get a tree," I smile.

"Oh, I am?"

I nod. "Uh-huh."

"And what if I don't want to?"

I shrug, turning to toss the dishcloth into the sink. I can see his reflection in the small window as I say, "If you don't, I'll find someone else."

His expression immediately sours. I bite my lip as he marches toward me, his body caging me in as he props his hands on the counter on either side of me. "What if I just handcuff you to my bed and have my way with you?"

His hips angle into mine, and I push right back against him. "Never letting me out? Your perfect little sex toy?" I ask playfully.

He nips at my ear. "I don't think you're supposed to sound that hot," he teases. He reaches up to give my low pigtail a tug. "You're too young for that kind of mind."

I knew what I was doing when I did my hair this morning. He hasn't been able to keep his hands off me. I smirk, taking in his words. I really don't know what has come over me. There's just something about my uncle that calls to that sexual beast inside of me. Maybe she wants out of her cage because she knows I'll just stuff her right back inside when life goes back to reality. "You bring it out," I tell him. "I think you're the only uncle I've ever…" I pretend to count on my hand like I've fucked another relation before, and he growls into my ear. I giggle in response, breaking free of his grip. "Come on, it'll be fun," I tell him, grabbing his hand.

He latches onto me, giving me a firm, brief squeeze like he doesn't want me to get away before he loosens his hold again. His forehead creases, so I only persist more, grabbing his hand and dragging him toward the swinging door.

I stop in the foyer to grab his winter hat. I pull it

down over my head and smile back at him. Next, I pull on the boots, and he only relents when I'm standing in front of the door, my hand around the doorknob.

He fishes the truck keys out of his pocket, and I almost squeal as we head outside. It's been days since we've been through the town again. Of course, I don't know which way he'll take me, but I hope it's through the snow-lined streets of Winterhaven.

He's quiet in the truck. The radio is on low, the carols of Christmas just barely audible above the truck's engine. When we get to the town, I turn it up a little until it feels like I'm in a real-life snow globe.

We're only a few blocks into town when he takes a right. The main street businesses turn into residences, and on the outskirts of that, I spy cars pulled over to the side of the road. "Where are we?" I ask, trying to see why everyone is parked here.

"The town Christmas fair."

I gasp. "There's a fair and you didn't tell me?"

He shrugs. "It's always going this time of year. This is where we get our Christmas trees."

He meets me in front of the truck, then takes out a pair of gloves from his pocket and hands them to me. "You didn't dress warm enough."

I pull them on happily, and we walk side-by-side to an area of white tents. A horse-drawn sleigh passes us. The driver waves to Cam, and he nods back. I just stare, watching the beautiful brown horses pull an actual sleigh. No wagon or spinning tires. The whole scene is backdropped by snow clinging to frost-bit trees. "It's beautiful," I tell him.

"They do it every year," he says in answer before steering me between a row of tents. There are people selling holiday crafts, hand-made toys, hot cocoa and Christmas cookies. At the far end of the lane, I spot green Christmas trees just beyond an arch that reads, *Winter Wonderland.*

Excitement pricks my skin. This is my first real Christmas tree. I grew up with fake, and since I'm usually at school right up until break, my parents already have theirs decorated before I get home.

I bite my lip, peering at all the holiday cheer, but it makes me wonder what happens when all of this is gone. "What's it like in the summer here?" I ask.

"Like this but greener."

I knock my shoulder into his. "You are a wealth of information."

He pulls away a little, and I note the distance he's put in between us as we walk under the arch.

"What kind of tree do you want?" he asks.

"What kind do you usually get?"

Before he can answer, a couple greets him. He talks with them pleasantly for a few minutes after introducing me as his niece, and then beelines straight for the last row of trees once they walk away.

I follow after him. Shoulders bunched, I watch as he takes in a deep breath. Then, someone else calls his name. The tension is right back as he turns, waving with a strained smile to the man on the other side of the row. I attempt to ask him what's wrong, but he turns away, intent on staring at our different options.

With a frown, I start looking at the trees too. Firs and pines. Some have different needles and slightly different shades of green. There are fat ones and skinny ones. Each one of them has the names written above in red lettering.

"Find one you like?" Uncle Cam asks finally.

I start, surprised he's even next to me. "They're all pretty. Any suggestions?"

Before he can answer, a female voice says, "Well, Cameron Michaels." I peer up to find a thirty-something year old woman with impossibly white teeth moving toward us. "I was hoping I would see you here. There's a tree over there that has your name all over it."

She wraps her arms around my uncle, and he doesn't seem surprised, although he's a little stiff as he hugs her back. I just stand there, feeling like the third wheel for a brief moment.

Pulling back, she beams at him until I start to fidget. "Who do we have here?" she asks.

"I'm Lilianne," I tell her, holding out my hand.

She gives it a quick shake. "Sophie. My family owns the tree farm."

My uncle clears his throat. "She's my—"

I glare at him. If he says niece, I'm going to lose it, but what are we then if we're not that? Is that the only description? He certainly can't say this is the girl he likes to fuck from behind.

Maybe coming out with him was a bad idea. Back at

the inn, everything seemed perfect for a brief moment. We didn't need labels, all we needed to know was that coming together felt good. Right, even.

She realizes he doesn't finish his thought and laughs, puffs of white smoke disappear into the air in front of her. "Be careful of this one," she warns me. "He's bound to make you fall in love and then ruin everything."

My stomach churns. Real fear grips me.

That better not be what's happening here. Love is not on my short term to-do list.

But when she walks away, threading her hand through the crook of his arm as she leads him to this perfect tree, I can't help the squeeze of jealousy that hits me.

There's definitely a story between these two—a past. I shouldn't care, but I do.

fourteen

. . .

SOPHIE'S BROTHERS help Cam put the tree in the back of the truck. I sit in the cab, stewing while rubbing my hands together as snow starts to fall outside again.

It's not the tree. It's perfect.

It's not even Sophie or the tinge of jealousy I felt.

I can't pinpoint exactly *why* this whole thing just freaking sucked.

Uncle Cam gets in, turning the heat up, and then drives away, the tree shifting a little in the back.

I stare at the beautiful white town as we roll through it. If Cameron Michaels was any other man, I'd have the right to get jealous. I'd be asking him right now what the deal is between him and Sophie. Hell, I'd even make him pull over so I can remind him that he likes to fuck me, not beautiful, tree-selling girls with bright pink cheeks.

Cam sighs next to me. "I told you it wasn't a good idea."

My muscles tense. "I know."

"I mean, what am I supposed to tell people?" he keeps going with exasperation. "'Hey, how'd you meet the girl you're fucking? Well, she's my stepsister's daughter.' It sounds like an episode of Jerry Springer."

I drop my head over my shoulder to look at him. "You just showed your age."

"And that's another thing," he says, really getting going now.

"Alright," I exclaim, trying to stop him from ranting. He's only reiterating the same things I've been saying in my head. Not to be overdramatic, but why is the world so cruel?

You know what, no. The world isn't cruel. It's proving a point. I need to finish school before I worry about a relationship. Uncle Cam is the perfect guy for me right now because in reality, nothing can ever come from it.

And as for right now, who cares what everyone else thinks? The only thing we're doing is fucking.

"Fine," I tell him. "No more going out of the inn as...whatever this is. Understood."

He peers over at me. Everything about his face tells me he's still concerned and unsure that I actually agree with him.

I give him a small, reassuring smile. "I'm hearing everything you're saying. But... that doesn't mean we have to stop, right? You like fucking me. I like fucking you. I'm mature enough to understand that this is what it is. No-strings attached. Two people who just enjoy one another."

He lifts a brow. "And when you go home it ends?"

"When my parents finally get here, it ends."

He holds out his hand, and I reach over to shake it. Except, he doesn't let me get that far, he peels off the glove he gave me and puts it back on his own hand. "Sounds like a plan."

I shake my head, giggling. "You're ridiculous. You want the other one, too?" I take that one off as well, throwing it at him. It drops in his lap, and he pulls that one on too.

However, my stare doesn't drift from his crotch. Maybe I do just want to prove a little bit that he likes fucking me more than Sophie. Or maybe I want to prove to him that I can be mature about this. Right? If it's all just for fun, what would I do right now?

Reaching over, I start to massage his dick through his pants.

He stills. "What are you…?"

"I have to keep my hands warm somehow. That was your master plan, wasn't it?"

He tightens his grip on the steering wheel, giving me a hard look, but then his face falters. "Fuck, baby girl," he grinds out, moving into my hand.

I take my seatbelt off, then move close, unbuttoning the clasp on his jeans and lowering his zipper. "I hope you can drive and get your dick sucked at the same time."

He lifts his hips in invitation, and I move his jeans

and boxers down to reveal his thick cock. With each stroke, it hardens even more in my hand, the tip glistening with precum.

"Don't tease me."

"Says the master of teasing."

"You enjoy the fuck out of it. Now put that pretty mouth on my cock."

I've never given head in a moving car before. A few days ago, I couldn't even say that I'd given head in a car before, but Uncle Cam popped both those cherries.

Bending over into the best position possible, I lick the cum off his tip. Uncle Cam makes a low growl in his throat as I take him down in the next instant, moving him into my mouth in one long stroke.

His fingers wind through my hair until he grips my roots. Even though he's driving, he sets the pace, pushing me over him and moving his hips up to help me take it all. "Suck me good. Like that," he groans. "You're too young to be this good."

His praise only makes me work harder, deeper. I want him to love this. I want him to think about me when I'm gone, jerk off to this memory. I know I'll be using my vibrator on overtime when I go back to school.

"Can you go all the way…?" he asks.

I open my mouth wider, and he pushes all the way to the hilt, hitting the back of my throat.

"That's it, Baby Girl. God, this is the perfect picture. Press those lips right into me. There you go. Fuck."

My whole body is on fire. My pussy clenches,

seeping juices into my panties.

"Oh, shit." He bucks into my mouth. Every hard ridge pushes past my lips as I lower on top of him. A breathy moan escapes as he forces me over him again.

He works his hand to the side of my head, pushing me away a little, so he can see his cock pulling from my mouth. Looking up, I watch as he flicks his gaze between me and the road. He lets me take over for a little while. Moving my hair, I keep this angle so he can watch me suck him. I focus on his tip, running my tongue all over and trying to suck him down like a thick milkshake.

He jerks. "Oh, fuck me." Grabbing my head again, he forces me over top of him until I take him all the way again. His movements become jerky. "I'm going to taint that perfect mouth of yours."

I moan.

"I'm going to fill it with my cum."

I'm absolutely drenched.

"Just…like…this," he says, pinpointing each word with strokes into my mouth. He lets out a masculine noise that has me clenching my thighs as he empties into my mouth. Cum hits the back of my throat, and I start swallowing on instinct. Swallowing and swallowing until he relaxes, shuddering his final release.

My eyelids flutter closed as I release him. I lick him one last time as I sit up, and his eyes have gone absolutely feral. Instead of scaring me, it thrills me to the core because I know I'm about to have a hell of a lot of fun with Uncle Cam again.

fifteen

. . .

YOU CAN'T DECORATE the tree without cookies and hot chocolate. It's tradition.

When I told Uncle Cam that, he only lifted his brows, but the man stuck around. I think he secretly loves having me here, and not just because of the other benefits.

He leaves briefly, only to return with Mrs. Williams. She gasps and cheers when she walks in. "Oh, I missed the baking we used to do in here." I peer between the two of them and catch it when she looks back at my uncle and puts on her best grandmotherly voice. "You should keep her around, Cameron. She's bringing the magic back." She comes swooping over to join me on the other side of the island and to my surprise, starts getting out her own mixing bowls. "Now..." She peers over at me while I stir chocolate chip cookie dough. "Oh, good. I'm making sugar cookies with my special frosting recipe. You're going to love them!"

She goes to work, and I can't help but peek up at Uncle Cam who's still standing in the doorway. He has a faraway look on his face, and if I'm not mistaken, a smile. A *genuine* smile. We lock gazes for a moment, and it deepens. His cheeks almost turning pink.

Turning, he props the kitchen doorway open, and from this vantage point, I can see through the dining room, through the hallway, all the way to where he's set up the tree in the sitting room in the corner. Mrs. Williams turns on the radio where Jingle Bells is in the middle of playing, and my body warms.

Now, *this* feels like Christmas. I miss Mom and Dad, sure, but that doesn't mean the spirit of the holiday is dead.

Mrs. Williams and I work side-by-side while my uncle finds every excuse to come into the room or walk by. He makes her laugh. "Okay, you vulture," she teases. "You know you want to come sample the batter."

He gives her a winning smile, and I watch their interaction with interest. I hadn't realized they knew one another all that well. I thought the Williams' were just guests, and maybe they are, but it seems like they've been guests for a while.

Uncle Cam comes over and swipes his finger through my cookie dough. He plops a ball into his mouth, his lids fluttering closed. They pop open a moment later, and he just stares at me. "They taste like June's."

Mrs. Williams reaches over to taste, too. "They

certainly do," she smiles, but it wanes. "Oh, but I miss her."

It goes silent for a moment. There's really nothing I can add. I miss the grandmother I used to know, but I don't know the woman they knew.

I swallow. My mom was hurt. I know this. But it wasn't right to keep me from her.

Mrs. Williams clears her throat. "Cameron, honey, will you please go get the mister? I need his stirring arm." She makes a muscle with her right arm that makes me smile.

Uncle Cam takes another scoop of my cookie dough before he leaves, avoiding my gaze. After he's gone, I peer up at my companion who's still looking at the empty doorway he just went through. She sighs. When she notices I'm staring at her, she perks up again. "By the way, I wanted to thank you for decorating our room."

"You're welcome," I tell her. "It wasn't much."

"It was enough. It reminded me of the old days."

"So, you stay here a lot over Christmas?" I ask because that's the only explanation I've been able to come up with.

"Oh, yes. For years." Her smile fades. "Cameron tries, but he wrestles with his own demons. Having his dreams taken away like that. Then his dad dies, then Miss June. I think this inn is simultaneously a gift and a… Well, like a prison for him."

My stomach clenches. I hadn't thought of it like that.

From what I'd thought, it made sense that he let the inn go because of his injury.

Mrs. Williams sets her mixing bowl and wooden spoon aside. Flour dust dots her arms. "You should've seen him before he got hurt. He'd try like the dickens to get here around the holidays. He loved your grandma's cookies," she says, nodding toward my own bowl. "He loved decorating. He'd help his dad with the exterior as he got older." She shakes her head. "With everything that happened so close together like that, I think he kind of lost himself."

She sighs again, looking off into space. I don't know what to say. Uncle Cam always has this hard persona. Like nothing gets to him. He's downright grumpy, actually.

"I'm glad he has some family here this year," Mrs. Williams says, grinning at me. "I wish your mom had been able to make it." I give her a look, and she throws her hands up. "I might be a bit of an eavesdropper. I'm just saying, he should have family around, even ones he's never met before."

"I agree," I tell her, taking a deep breath. If I wasn't here, I really don't know what he would have done. He couldn't even handle one breakfast.

She elbows me in the arm. "And I knew you looked like your Grandma. I bet your mom is the spitting image."

The entrance of Mr. Williams clapping his hands together and rubbing them saves me from answering. "I hear I'm needed."

Mrs. Williams gestures towards her bowl. "Right here. I hope you've been working on your exercises."

Immediately, Mr. Williams walks over, picks up the tune of the carol on the radio and starts whistling. Cam is leaning against the doorjamb, and I lock gazes with him. He doesn't take his eyes off me, and neither one of us looks away until Mrs. Williams elbows me again. "You better get your cookies in the oven."

"Right," I say, laughing. I start looking around for cookie tins when Cam moves forward, grabbing a few from a cupboard and setting them on the island for me.

"I recommend this one," he says, moving a flat one forward. "June thought it was magic."

sixteen

. . .

THE SMELL of hot chocolate lingers in the air.

Mrs. Williams made it from scratch. A recipe that my grandmother gave her, apparently. As soon as I tasted it, it was familiar. Like a forgotten memory come to life.

I'm full of sugar, skin buzzing with all the cookies I've eaten—and topped off with a bite of alcohol. Uncle Cam invited all the guests down to trim the tree and broke out several bottles of wine along with a bottle of Kahlua to top off our hot chocolate. I might have found my new favorite drink.

There's laughter all around. Conversation flows easily.

By the time the guests start retreating to their rooms, it's past ten o'clock. The tree is absolutely beautiful. It isn't one of those trees that's color-themed or put up with design in mind. It's homey. Bulbs that have a history. There's a tiny sleigh with my mom's name on it. Her "baby ornament" with the year of her birth printed on the side. Ornaments with pictures of Uncle Cam from when he was a kid, or fun Christmas crafts he'd made in his younger years that weren't perfect in the least, but actually *are* perfect because they tell a story.

I sit back on the couch, another hot chocolate in my hand as I stare at the tree. It doesn't look like my mom's tree, but that's okay, it's still somehow feels right. Every once in a while, I get a whiff of pine over the chocolate, and my heart is happy.

Uncle Cam returns to the room with a bag of marshmallows. He turns the light off until it's just the fire from the fireplace and the tree lights lighting the room. "Here," he says. "I thought you could use more of these."

I fill my cup up with the mini marshmallows again and drop the bag on the side table to my left. He sits next to me, placing his hand on my leg. He's grabbed a beer from the kitchen and sips it while staring at the tree.

"That was fun," he finally says, his voice low, almost mimicking the magic in the air. "It reminded me of old times."

"I haven't helped decorate the tree in years," I tell him. "I'm always at school when Mom puts it up." I snicker as a thought pops into my head, and it's then I realize it's possible I'm a little tipsy. "I especially liked the ornament of you in second grade." I start laughing and can't stop. He squeezes my leg, staring down at me with a huge grin.

"Is it the hair?" he asks.

I nod, still chuckling. I set my hot chocolate down so I can mimic his spiky hair with my hands. "It's so pointy."

He laughs deep in his chest, and it's baritone-like. "It was the style."

"Sure, sure," I tell him. "Says everyone who wants to get out of their bad hair choices."

"I don't know. I was pretty slick as an eight-year-old," he says, puffing out his chest. "I think I had two girlfriends that day."

"Ooh, big man on campus."

"Yep," he says taking a swig of his beer. "I rocked the halls of BCA."

My chest actually rattles with laughter. "I was a dork," I inform him. "I don't think I had my first boyfriend, if you can even call it that, until I was a senior."

"So, what you're telling me is that you're second grade ornament looks worse than mine."

"Oh, a hundred percent, which is why you'll never see it."

He turns toward me. "Well, that's not fair."

The amount of Kahlua coursing through me must loosen my lips. "Think teacher's pet with glasses, and a crooked smile." I give him the widest smile I can with my teeth pressed firmly together before I break into a fit of laughter again.

He laughs with me. "If it looks anything like that, it's adorable."

I grab my hot cocoa, trying to steady my hands so I

don't spill it. The new marshmallows have melted, and I slurp them off the top before taking another drink.

"You really like school then, huh?" he asks.

Shrugging, I say, "Yeah, I guess. I like that there's always an answer for everything. My mom is a free spirit, and I crave structure. Don't get me wrong, I love her to death, but I swear the woman can't leave the house on time to save her life. She never knows where her purse is. Her keys."

"And you're the exact opposite."

"Yep," I say, popping the "p" proudly.

He leans back, taking another drink of his beer. The tree lights light up his face in distinct colors. "I was like that for a long time. You have to have a strict schedule to play professionally. Eating, working out, studying, practice, team meetings. I even scheduled downtime."

I raise my brows, but I don't know why. I do the absolute same. On Saturdays, I read a book for two hours, and that's what I call my "me" time.

"It's exhausting," he says, peering over at me.

"But worth it," I say with a smile, holding up my mug.

He clicks his beer glass against it and nods. "Totally worth it."

He looks away, face somber as he stares at the lights. I join him, snuggling into his side, and gaze at the tree until my eyes close.

seventeen

. . .

I AWAKE TO A FOREIGN FEELING. Blinking, I wait until my eyes come into focus. Bending over me is Uncle Cam. He's tracing his fingers over my cheeks with a smile on his face. I turn over, stretching, still blissfully in my morning haze until I see him with a towel around his hips, his naked chest on full display.

"Hey," he says. "If you don't wake up now, the guests are going to be forced to eat whatever disastrous concoction I come up with."

I shoot up in bed, and he has to jump back. My stare lingers over the unfamiliar things in this room. It doesn't look like the other rooms. It's actually lived in, personalized. "Am I in your room?" I practically gasp.

He chuckles. "You fell asleep on me last night, and I...didn't want to carry you up the stairs."

"I slept in your bed?" I ask, unable to believe it.

"Is that okay?"

It hits me then that I didn't once wake up in the

middle of the night. I slept like a baby. It could've been the alcohol. *Yeah, probably the alcohol.* I whip the sheets off me. "Yeah, fine. Absolutely fine."

My toes dig into the plush area rugs surrounding his bed. There's a dresser in the corner with a book titled, "Walking Miracle" on the top. I run my fingers over it as Uncle Cam retreats to his closet on the opposite side of the room. His room is well-kept and clean. Instead of the country decor in the rest of the house, his sheets are dark blue, almost silky to the touch.

Uncle Cam drops the towel, and my stare immediately finds his muscled ass. Despite the fact that he doesn't play professionally anymore, he's still in amazing shape.

"You can use my shower," he calls out over his shoulder. "I'll run to get some clothes from your room." He pulls on a pair of boxers and turns, catching me staring at him. "Just tell me what you want." He quirks his lips.

"Yeah, um." I make myself look away. "Just a pair of jeans and that gray sweater I have? Everything should be put away in the dresser."

Reaching behind him, he grabs his own pair of jeans and starts pulling them on. "Great. I'll be right back down." He picks out a collared shirt from the hangers before leaving the room. He's still pulling it on as the door closes behind him. I let out a breath, but then the door opens again. "I forgot," he says, smiling in at me. "Merry Christmas Eve."

Merry Christmas Eve? How is it almost Christmas

already? Nothing's the same as previous years, but this also feels so good. "Merry Christmas Eve," I respond, stomach clenching. Yesterday must have done him some good. He's…happy.

He shuts the door, and I immediately head into the shower. By the time I'm done, my clothes are laid out on his made bed. I can smell bacon seeping in from under the door, so I hurry and change. I dry my hair as much as I can, thinking the whole time about how I can't believe he let me in his bed. I slept next to him.

The only bad thing about it is that I don't remember it at all.

Uncle Cam and I cook breakfast for the guests. Everyone is in happy spirits, just like last night. Mrs. Williams proposes we all go to the Christmas fair, and instead of balking at the idea, Uncle Cam agrees.

I guess miracles really do happen during Christmas.

The older woman winks at me. "They don't put Kahlua in their hot chocolate, but it's still good."

"Oh, calling me out, are we? That's not very festive," I tease.

"Festive was the way you were singing 'Deck the Halls' at the top of your lungs last night," the man from the second couple jokes.

All I can do is laugh. He's not wrong. I playfully cringe. "So, are we all agreeing that I shouldn't drink today?"

"No," Mr. Williams says. "Please do. That was the most fun I've had in a long time."

His wife reaches over to grasp his hand, then pulls

out a present from her lap. "Lilianne, I have this for you."

I take the present from her. Green paper with snowmen all over stare back at me as I peer at it. My heart squeezes. "Thank you," I tell her.

"It's nothing much," she says as I open it, pulling out a royal blue knitted hat. "I noticed you didn't have one."

"Wow, this is…" I peer into her eyes. "Thank you," I tell her, pulling the hat over my head. "It fits perfectly."

She gets up with the rest of the guests, and I give her a hug. "You're welcome. I don't want to see you catch your death out there today."

I smile as she pulls away. Cam tells them we'll leave in ten minutes if everyone is okay with that. They all agree, and I find myself waiting outside in the snow with my cute hat, my hands shoved into my jacket, and my heart full as Cam pulls around in a big white van with the words, *Winterhaven Shuttle* scrawled across the side. The i in Winterhaven is dotted with an elf's head, the t is a stocking, and the a and e are Mr. and Mrs. Claus respectively. It's positively adorable.

Uncle Cam gets out to hold the passenger door open for me. "Come on in."

I start that way, and he gives my butt a squeeze as I get in. "Where did this come from?"

"It's the inn's shuttle," he tells me, shrugging like he's been using it this entire time. This inn must have been really something.

He helps the rest of the guests into the back, and

then we're on our way. The snow sparkles with the sun's rays bouncing off it. It's cold enough to see my breath, but the shuttle's heat is working just fine, so it's toasty inside.

At the fair, everyone is smiling and waving. I shop from booth to booth, mostly looking at all the crafts. Of course, I get a hot cocoa and sip it, and surprisingly, Uncle Cam doesn't leave my side. He doesn't shy away when people come near. He points out different things, and it's almost as if we're learning each other. He finds out I love reindeer, and every time my hot cocoa runs out, he brings me another.

We stop and watch a snowman making competition. There are games, too. Kids throwing snowballs at targets where they win stuffed animals with red scarves or a blow-up reindeer, or a package of candy canes.

We walk around for so long that my stomach starts growling. We stop and eat at the Wonderland Eatery and then make our rounds again until we end up near the road when a carriage passes. Uncle Cam nudges me. "Do you want to go for a ride?"

"Really?"

"I saw you eyeing them up last time."

"I would love to," I tell him, a little astonished.

He flags down the driver, calling him Harry, who tells him he has an opening next if we want to hop on.

My heart leaps in my chest as Uncle Cam helps me into the sleigh. There's a holder for my hot cocoa and a white and red checkered wool blanket that Cam pulls onto our laps.

"Here we go," Harry says, clucking at the horses until they take off.

Cam puts his arm around me, pulling me close. I'm in awe of how open he's being, but I'm quickly distracted when white flakes start falling from the sky. They're few and far between. Just a dusting. "This is so cool," I say as Harry navigates the horses through the streets of Winterhaven. People walking the sidewalks all wave to us until we come out the other side of the small town and pull into a field where I can tell the horses have been before. Up ahead, there's an opening in the forest, and the tracks lead that way. Straight through a true winter wonderland. Undisturbed snow clinging to branches. Iced over ponds. It's breathtaking.

Cam takes his arm off my shoulders and instead, places it on my thigh. He traces his thumb back and forth over my jeans, and I don't even realize he's doing it until he moves higher and higher. He caresses the area just below my apex, and I sit back, dragging my gaze away from the beautiful scene in front of me to his mischievous green eyes. He leans over and whispers, "I hope you can be quiet."

With the blanket still firmly over our laps, he deftly unzips my jeans with one hand, unclasping my button, and cups me within moments. I press my lips together to keep from moaning. *Is he serious?* I eye Harry's back. He hasn't turned around once, and even if he had, the blanket is there, right?

Right, I tell myself because there's no way I'm stopping Uncle Cam from what he's doing. He reaches inside my jeans, and I shift to help, moving my jeans down a little to give him freedom of movement as he pries my legs apart and circles my clit over my panties.

I grab his arm, holding on to it as he watches my every movement. My breath hitches. There's a tightness in my chest, a restraint. I don't want to call attention to what we're doing, but damn, I want more.

He leans over. "You're so beautiful, baby girl. I couldn't help myself." He nips at my ear. "I was jealous of the trees. You kept looking at them like you were in awe, but I'm used to you looking at me like that."

I'm flustered and wet. I open my legs wider, and he takes the opportunity to slip under my panties, working my juices over my folds until he slips his finger inside.

I jerk into him, and he smiles against the shell of my ear. "If you keep quiet, I'll give you a present later."

With the sultry tone in his voice, I know exactly the kind of gift he wants to give me, and I'm all in.

"Have I told you how much I love this pussy?" he whispers. I angle my hips up, and he drives his finger inside me again, swirling and stroking in perfect harmony.

"When you come, I want to feel you squeeze me. Can you do that?"

I nod, eagerly. My gaze darts to Harry, but Cam nips at my ear again.

"Eyes on me. I want to see your face when you lose it."

He keeps up his rhythm, and my whole body locks with tension. I rock into him when I can. The horse whinnies up ahead. The clop, clop of their hooves on the packed snow covers up any noises that slip through my lips.

Up ahead, I spot the opening in the trees, and I know I need to come before then. I can't have Uncle Cam's finger inside me as we go back through Winterhaven, fingering me while we wave.

"Baby girl, you're running out of time. Will you come for me?"

Fuck me. Fuck me.

He rubs my clit with the palm of his hand, and every single sensation works me even higher. I move my hand down, gripping his wrist, moving him against me until my body coils up tight. My lips part on a silent scream as I orgasm. My pussy squeezes his finger again and again while I soak not only his hand but my panties as well.

My breath comes out in gasps and stutters, and all the while, he leans over me, "That's my girl. You feel so fucking good." He quirks his finger inside me, sending me into another round of spasms as I grip his thigh with my free hand.

Evil, evil man.

eighteen

. . .

THERE'S something about the night before Christmas. It's as if magic hangs from invisible strings in the sky, and that star-like wonder just dangles right in front of you like you're in a mystical galaxy where all there is is love and light.

Cam and I sit on the couch in the sitting room again, the fire crackling. After dinner, all of the guests hung out for a while before dispersing to their different rooms to spend the evening with their loved ones alone. I even spoke to my mom and dad on the phone while cooking dinner, but all of that fades as Cam takes my face in his hands. He's been staring at me all evening, sneaking in short touches, and that fire in his eyes is back at this very moment.

The fireplace warmth makes my cheeks heat. But another kind of heat threads through my veins, tangling me up in knots. "I was hoping they would go to bed," he murmurs, glancing at my lips.

His voice has a brush of breathiness to it as he stares over every inch of my face. He tucks my hair behind my ear and wraps his strong hands around the back of my neck, pulling me in close.

My heart thunders. He's going to kiss me.

This man has had his dick in my mouth, in my pussy from behind, and I've straddled him to ecstasy, but this—this right here turns my insides to goo. His hot breath washes over my lips, and my eyes flutter closed.

Nothing happens for what seems like forever, then his lips brush mine hesitantly. An instant hunger takes over me. I move close, sealing my lips to his like I can't get enough. The truth is, I can't get enough. His tongue prods, and I open for him. Fully. Completely. He sweeps into my mouth with an urgency that has me moaning into his mouth. We kiss and kiss like we're making up for lost time. There was no kissing before. Just pure passion wrapped up in the act, but this is something more.

Cameron Michaels has a hold of me. His grumpy ass has his claws sunk into my heart, and when a man kisses like this—with his whole body—I have half a mind to think I've done the same to him, too.

He pulls me onto his lap, and I settle over him, still kissing him like we're pre-teens getting away with something. And maybe that's exactly what we are doing.

I break away, needing to take a moment, and he

kisses down my throat. The words coming out of his mouth make me feel like butter. Rich, beautiful, loved.

"Cameron…" I breathe out, and I don't even have to express what I want in words.

He gets up, taking me with him. I wrap my legs around his waist while we kiss all the way to his room. Desperate, lingering kisses that share what our thoughts can't. I'm a one-minded grad student with a perfection problem, and he's a broken ex-NFL player with a bad attitude, but we just work. Nothing is more testament to that than the last twenty-four hours.

He leans me against his closed door, his fingers digging into my hips. "Fuck. What are you doing to me, Lilianne?"

I bite my lip, watching him watch me with the most awed expression that nearly turns everything in me over and rearranges it into something new.

He works my zipper down, then sets me on my feet, so he can push my jeans down my legs. I work on his next, and they follow mine to the floor. He slips his hand into my panties, teasing my folds. "Cameron…" I moan again, but this time, it's more like a warning. We both know he can make me come with just his fingers, but I want more than that this time. Whatever this is has been building and building.

He pulls his hand free then yanks the shirt over my head, leaning into me so that his chest meets mine. I work on his next, until we're skin-to-skin. He kisses me one last time, stealing my breath, before leading me to the bed. While I stare, he pulls the boxers I saw him put on this morning down, revealing his hard, thick cock.

I lie down, wiggling out of my panties. Before I can work on my bra, he crawls over me, settling in all the right places. He takes his time removing my remaining piece of clothing. He kisses the skin over my bra cups before reaching underneath my body. Even when he has my clasps undone, he only pulls bits of the fabric away a little at a time, searching lower and lower with his mouth. After he reveals my nipples, he still takes it slow before he's licking the curve of my breasts, then the center of my breasts as he cups me.

He shifts over me, and he's right there, angling toward my center. I spread my legs to welcome him inside. Even though he'd made me orgasm earlier, I want more of this. More intimacy. More…caring. I want the feel of his dick sliding in and out of me in perfect thrusts.

Again, he takes his time. Instead of diving right in, he uses his magical fingers to work me up. It isn't until I'm breathing heavy and pleading with, "Cameron Michaels, please push your cock inside me right now," that he complies.

He hovers above me, his fingers flexing into the pillow behind my head. He gives me slow, languid strokes while I stare at his chest, my body quivering underneath him.

It's then that I realize this isn't fucking. This is something more. Something that twists my insides up.

He tilts my chin up to meet his gaze and claims my

mouth at the same time he slams into me. His kiss silences my groan, but goosebumps spread over my arms.

"You're kind of perfect," he says, holding my hips in place as he rocks into them slowly again.

I'm almost afraid to speak because there's an emotion crawling up my throat that I don't want to voice yet, so instead, I smirk, "Says the man with the six-pack."

"It was eight last time I checked."

"Silly me. And I'm supposed to have a college degree."

A soft smile comes to his lips as sweat dots his forehead. Leaning over, he kisses me again, and we spend the whole time tasting and soothing until my body starts to shake. A slow burn has turned into an oncoming tsunami. "Cameron," I pant.

He drops his forehead to mine, keeping the same pace until I spasm around him. My pleasure comes out in a gasp, like falling over a cliff. The exhilaration comes next. Only fueled by the fact that he comes seconds after me. The groan that releases from his throat is sexy as hell, his dick releasing inside of me.

I breathe out, but immediately breathe in fear. That was the best sex I've ever had. Not only that, but when he pulls back to stare at me, I *feel* things. My heart leaps. I can barely breathe.

It's possible I've fallen too far for him. Way too far.

nineteen

. . .

"LILIANNE?"

I stir in my sleep. Even through the haze, I can feel myself smile. Last night was…amazing. Cam grabs my hips, pulling me back against him. I kept waking up in the middle of the night to feel his arms tightly around me. I was awake when it crossed midnight, making it officially Christmas. I've always had a hard time sleeping on Christmas, but this year was something else.

"Are you awake?" he whispers.

"I am now," I say, turning toward him.

He smiles, then reaches behind him.

"You're dressed?" I ask, noticing he's wearing a proper button-up shirt and nice jeans. His hair is styled. He's so ready for the holiday, and I'm still not wearing any clothes.

"I couldn't sleep much. I had to get up and take pain reliever last night."

However, there's no distress on his face as he offers me a steaming cup of coffee. I breathe in deep, smelling the rich aroma. "You, Sir, are an angel," I tease as I sit up in bed and take the mug from him.

"Also…" He reaches behind him again. This man is a magician. He keeps pulling things out, but what he presents me with this time is wrapped in an oblong box.

I stare at the wrapping paper, then at him. "You got me a present?"

He shrugs. "It's no big deal."

The hell it isn't. This is a huge deal. I frown as I take it from him. "I didn't get you anything."

"Trust me, I unwrapped my present last night… several times," he grins.

I chuckle, shaking my head. "That was fun, wasn't it?" I ask, leaning over to peck him on the lips. He deepens the kiss immediately. If there was any doubt on my part that last night was a fluke, this proves it wasn't. I dig my nails into his arm to hold on.

Eventually, he stops the kiss before it goes any further and motions toward the present. "Open it."

He's smiling from ear-to-ear, so I tear the present open to find a black-topped box. Flipping the lid, I grin. A reindeer charm bracelet sits inside. It's the same one I'd admired yesterday at one of the craft booths in the winter fair. "You didn't," I gasp, peering at him.

"I could tell you liked it and everyone should open up something on Christmas."

He takes it out of the box and puts it on me. Holding

it up, I twist my wrist to see how it glints in the light. "It's beautiful. Thank you."

More and more, I wonder how I'm going to leave this man. It's just supposed to be a fling. Especially because he's my step-uncle, but also because we both have other lives. I have to go back to school. He has to run the inn. Those physical locations aren't near each other, and of course, there's also that problem that he doesn't actually want anything from this. At least, that's what he'd said, but it seems like so many things have changed.

"Cameron—"

My phone starts ringing. I peer over to see my mom's face, and my stomach clenches. She's video chatting me. Reaching over, I pull on the sweater I had on yesterday and then grab my phone. As soon as I can see her on the screen, I say, "Merry Christmas!"

"Merry Christmas!" She and Dad say at the same time.

"I wish you were with us," Mom says, pouting.

Cameron sneaks off the bed. You can clearly see the pillows and headboard behind me, so I suppose it would be a bad thing if he video chatted with me. I'm sure that would stir up questions.

"Speaking of that," my father says. The phone shakes as he takes it. "Mom and I want to buy you a plane ticket so you can fly home tomorrow. Flights are going in and out again."

"Oh," I say, gaze darting toward Cam. He's standing

by the side of the bed facing away from me. "You're not flying out here?"

"We got thinking about it, and Christmas is over. I'd rather come in the summer, so we don't have to deal with all the flight issues."

My mouth goes dry. "But Grandma Junie," I retort. "Plus, it's really beautiful in the winter. Cam—Uncle Cam took me to the winter fair, and the town is so—"

"Won't they be taking all that down soon though?" Mom asks. "I mean, the holiday is practically over."

I glance toward Cameron. He's not even looking at me. He's just standing there. I can't see his face. I can't tell what he's feeling. Or thinking. Nothing. As for me, I'm freaking out. I'm suddenly faced with reality, and I don't want to be. "I mean, probably," I tell her. "But I have no idea."

"Oh," my dad says. He reaches out of view of the camera and brings up a letter. It takes several tries, but he finally gets it centered in front of the screen. "This came for you." It's a letter from my school. "Do you want us to open it?"

"Sure," I say, biting my lip. My skin feels like it's crawling. This isn't how I wanted this morning to go down. Now, my parents aren't coming. They're talking about me leaving, which we were *all* supposed to be leaving in a few days anyway, but that was before all of this happened. I'd put leaving out of my mind the last couple of days.

Dad gets the letter open and starts reading. "It says

something about a TA position. Congratulations, you've been selected to—" he starts to read.

"You're kidding!" I shout, my body vibrates for a completely different reason. I'd almost forgotten I'd applied for that teaching assistant position because I thought it was a longshot.

"Nope," my father says, pushing his glasses back up his nose. "It's from a Professor Warren."

"Oh my God," I say, kicking my feet and smiling. He's one of the most decorated professors in my department. *This is amazing!*

I peer over at Cameron to see that he's finally turned to stare at me. He has a soft smile on his face, but it looks sad.

I take a deep breath to calm myself down.

This is good. Great even, so why do I feel like shit right now?

twenty

. . .

CAM HASN'T ASKED me if I'm going home yet. I dodged about ten calls from my mom because I'm sure she wants an answer. Christmas day was full of this strained sort of co-existence between him and me. We laughed. We joked. We made dinner together and fed the guests a proper Christmas meal, but there was this underlying talk that needs to be had that kept everything just short of perfect.

Football was on the TV all day. And I mean *all* day. Watching him watch football was an experience. He said words I didn't even know existed. His passion for the game is certainly still there.

Later that night, he took me to bed again, but as I feel the bed next to me now, the sun's rays shining in through the window, he's not here. There's no morning coffee or feeling him pull me tight to his chest. However, I can sniff out bacon, which is odd since the last time he attempted to make bacon all by himself, he burnt the crap out of it.

I force myself to get out of bed. My brain feels like mush. After checking my phone, I see that my mom has already called me this morning. I'm stuck. Half of me wants to stay. Half of me wants to go. Since I got this TA position, it's possible they'll want me to return to campus early. I might only have days.

I know what I need to do. I know what old Lilianne would do, but I'm procrastinating. I'm…just not into it.

Hurrying in the shower, I get ready in record time and speed walk to the kitchen with my hair still wet. I push the door open and stop in my tracks. A woman stands in the kitchen cutting up potatoes. She glances up, and I recognize her as the cook who was leaving the first day I got here. "Good morning, Honey. I'll have breakfast right out."

"Oh, I'm not—" I cut myself off. I was going to say, I'm not a guest, but is that what I am now? "I'm Cameron's niece," I tell her, and my tongue feels like it's stuck to the roof of my mouth, not wanting the words to come out. These last couple of days, I was so much more, and it felt so right.

"That's right," she says happily. "I forgot you would be here. You're the one who must have helped him through things here because Lord knows he wouldn't have been able to do it himself." She laughs softly to herself and shakes her head. "Well, this morning, you get to have me do it all, so why don't you go take a seat at one of the tables?"

She's just trying to be nice, but for some reason, it feels like she stabbed a knife into my gut. Turning, I walk back into the dining room. The door swings closed, and I stare at the empty tables, almost lost.

When I hear footsteps out in the hallway, my gaze snaps up, and in walks Cameron Michaels. He takes off his hat and gloves and sets them on the entryway table. He was probably out chopping wood again. Turning, he finds me staring at him, and he takes a deep breath before walking forward. His stare takes me in, but it seems guarded. He shoves his hands into his pockets. "So, what time are you leaving?"

I blink at him, and my heart sinks. "Leaving?"

He shrugs. "School. TA. Your mom."

My fingers flex at my sides. "Right. And you've got your cook back."

He swallows, mostly staring down at his feet. "Yeah, she showed up this morning. Her husband is feeling much better."

"Well, that's great," I tell him, trying to be happy, even though that's the last thing I feel. I don't even really like to cook, but it was just being here. Hell, who am I kidding? It was being here *with him.* It was experiencing all of this *with him.*

He clears his throat. "We said this was just a thing. A small, short thing." It's as if he can't even bring himself to say the words. *Thing* doesn't encompass what we did. We were supposed to be two people who just liked to fuck one another, but it turned into so much more. And he knows it. At least, I thought he did.

Maybe this is his way of letting me know he's done. He had his fun. The kissing didn't actually mean anything. Nor did the fact that he took me to town without reservation. The present… It was all just him playing at I don't know what.

"Right. That's what we said." I wait for him to say something else. Anything else. But the longer he takes, the more distance it puts between us. I don't even know what I expected. He told me what this was from the start, and it's not like I don't have to go home. "That's it, then?" I ask, and I kind of hate myself for trying to beg him to say *something.* An *I'll miss you*. An *I had fun,* might help this sting a little less.

"Yeah," he says, and his voice cuts out. He clears his throat. "Yeah, I think so."

twenty-one

. . .

MOM PUSHES play on the movie. Since we didn't get to watch White Christmas together this year, she'd thought we'd do it, even if it is five days post-Christmas and I really don't have any Christmas spirit left in me. I left that back with Cam.

I sip the hot chocolate she made me. Marshmallows dot the top, but it doesn't have Kahlua, so it's automatically inferior.

"Your Grandma loved this movie," Mom muses.

I turn toward her. "Really? You never told me that."

She shrugs then pulls the lap blanket she has stretched over her up. "Well, I didn't talk about her much, did I?"

"No," I say, and I'm pretty sure it comes out with too much attitude because she peeks over at me with her brows raised. "You would've really liked it there, Mom," I tell her, thinking about the inn. I swear I haven't stopped thinking about the inn. I understand why Grandma Junie wanted to share it with us. Why she sent the pictures and the letters. "It was like a movie." Of course, my time spent with Cameron Michaels flick by too, but that's more like an X-rated television show. I can't think of the inn without thinking of him though.

"I wish the flights hadn't been canceled."

"You should really go," I urge her. "And Cameron... Uncle Cameron. You'll like him."

She blows out a breath. I can tell that she still wrestles with my grandmother's decisions even though she forgave her. However, my mom wasn't exactly trying for all those years either. She broke ties with her completely. "I'm going to go," she insists. "I will. I just wish we hadn't decided to go over Christmas because now I completely missed spending Christmas with you, and you have to go back to school soon."

I reach over, and she puts her hand in mine, squeezing it. "I know." I wrestle with what to say, but I swear if I don't actually push her to go, she won't. She'll just keep coming up with excuses. "Uncle Cameron lost everything, you know. His career, his dad, then Grandma. I think you might be the only family he has left, and I missed you and Dad, but I'm also glad I was there with him. I doubt he would've spent Christmas with anybody special otherwise."

She frowns. "That is a terrible way to spend a holiday."

My stomach clenches. I wonder what he's doing right now. If he's thinking about me like I'm thinking about him. Maybe he was able to go back to his normal life. A fling with a young girl that he could just forget. However, it's not as if he can forget me either. We are kind of related. "I got the feeling that Grandma did a lot for him. I bet you would enjoy talking to him about things. Did you know Grandma kept your baby ornament? I hung it on the tree myself."

Mom's lip quivers. In the background, Bing Crosby sings "White Christmas." "I know I'm being judgmental," she relents. "The heart wants what it wants, but she just left Dad behind." She sighs. "I forgive her. I do."

"You should," I tell her. "You made her accountable for a very long time but look at what you missed out on."

She squeezes my hand again and gives me a watery smile. "I know. It's just hard for me to think that maybe Dad wasn't the one for Mom because they had me. Why wouldn't it be Dad?" She shakes her head. "I guess you never know about love. It's strange and works in weird ways. You'll find out someday."

I turn toward the screen as a sharp pain hits my chest. I miss Cam. I even miss the grumpy and surly parts of him. I miss the way he'd call me smart mouth even though I secretly think he'd grown to love it.

The heart wants what it wants…

Suddenly, I think I know exactly how Grandma felt

when she left Grandpa. Too bad my story won't end the same way.

The man I'll be comparing every other man to doesn't see me like that, or I'd be faced with a very difficult decision.

twenty-two

. . .

MY "YOU'RE-GOING-TO-BE-REALLY-LATE" alarm sounds on my phone. I hop up and down to put my shoes on as I scramble to the door of my apartment. I have my keys in my mouth as I twist the knob. This TA position has been kicking my ass. I already know I'm going to get a lecture from Professor Warren, but if the man would let me fucking sleep, I wouldn't always be scrambling around like a chicken with my head cut off.

I whip the door open and stop in my tracks. A man stands outside my door, and when I open it, he turns. "Cam," I gasp, the keys falling from my mouth and hitting the floor.

My body vibrates, shock ricochets through me.

He swoops down to grab my keys and stands to his full height. He's wearing a black coat over a dark blue shirt, coupled with his nice jeans.

"Is this a bad time?" he asks sheepishly.

I open my mouth to answer. The rational part of my brain is screaming yes. Yes, it's a very bad time. I'm already late, but this is Cameron Michaels. The man's name I've been crying out for weeks as I drain my vibrator's batteries. "I'm…"

"It is," he says. "You're clearly going somewhere."

"No," I find myself saying. "No, I just regularly jump up and down in my hallway and open the door up randomly."

He smirks, and it nearly takes my breath away. God, he's so fucking hot. My memories of him didn't do this man justice. I even put football on in the background while I do work now, just so I can hear him yell in my head.

After handing me my keys, he fidgets. "I came here to say a few things, but mainly, I just wanted to do this." He steps forward, threading his hands through my hair before kissing me in one smooth motion that I don't even see it coming. He pins me to him, his mouth searching, his tongue delving deep as he nearly brands me with the ferocity of his kiss. I melt into him, getting caught up in the wave that is Cameron Michaels.

God, this. This is what I missed.

A few seconds pass before he pulls away. "I thought so," he mumbles to himself. He moves in, closing the door behind him like he owns the place, and I move out of the way as he walks into my apartment. He starts to pace, and when he looks up, I'm still in the hallway. "What are you doing? Get over here."

I walk toward him slowly. He's ran his hands

through his hair until it's sticking up adorably. I'm still trying to process the fact that he's here. I'm… I'm shocked. That's it. I'm in shock.

When I get to him, he reaches for my hand. "I hired a new housekeeper," he smiles, and I almost choke. I had no idea he'd be leading off with that.

That's what he came all this way to tell me? "That's g—"

"I implemented an online reservation system," he adds. "I made an appointment to get the inn painted, and I have a guy coming out next week to seal up the windows." He squeezes my hand. "I did all these things because I could hear your voice in my head, telling me what needed to be done. I really liked hearing that voice. You made me fall in love with the inn again, Lilianne. You made me think about life differently."

"Shit, shit," he says, staring at me with uncertainty. "I told myself I was just going to come here, I was just going to show up to see what happened. I mean, I hadn't even gotten the courage to knock on your door yet…" he says, his words coming out in a rush.

"You want to go back out?" I ask with a smile.

He grins, shaking his head. After a brief moment, he locks gazes with me again. "There's something you need to understand about me. For so long, things just kept getting taken away. My career, my parents. I lost everything that was making me whole…and then you—a girl who was just supposed to be a one-night stand—looked up at me at the airport, and you changed my whole damn life."

I suck in a breath. Goosebumps thread through me from head to toe. He steps into me, putting his arms around my shoulders, and it's as easy as breathing. We fit together like two random puzzle pieces that aren't even from the same set, but somehow, it just works. We just work.

"Cameron…"

He smiles at me. "You made me remember that when the game throws you an obstacle, you just find a different path. You can't hesitate. You can't think. The truth is, I was scared, Lilianne."

I lift my brows, shocked to hear him say that.

"I knew I would screw it up because everything else got screwed up, but it was a self-fulfilling prophecy. That's exactly what happened, and I've been hating myself ever since I dropped you off at the airport. Listen, I don't care what we are to each other because the only thing we are to each other that matters is the fact that I want to be around you like this," he says, gripping me. "You make me better. I've been losing my mind back at the inn."

I smile at his words. My stomach twists. I have to shut my mind off because it keeps wanting to work through a problem. I'm at school. He's in Maine. How will we make it work? But I tell my brain to take a vacation as I pull him close. "You're damn right I make you better."

He chuckles, sealing his lips to mine once more. He lifts me up, and I wrap my legs around his waist. "Is that a yes?" he asks.

"Did you even ask me a question?"

His whole chest vibrates with laughter. "I guess I'm asking if you like me."

"Do I like you?" I hide my smiling face in the crook of his neck. "I don't think any respectable woman lets a man put his dick inside her unless she at least likes him."

"There's that smart mouth again." His eyes dance with amusement.

"It never stops," I echo, and then I kiss him again, telling him with my lips what I want to say because I told my brain to take a hike, and I have no idea how to express to him that yes, I want nothing more than to be in his life like this.

Wrapped up in one another.

Embracing one another.

Until it's just too difficult to figure out where he ends and I begin.

The heart wants what it wants, right? The rest of the stuff, we'll figure out in time.

As long as we're together, that's what matters.

About the Author

E. M. Moore is a USA Today Bestselling author of Contemporary and Paranormal Romance. She's drawn to write within the teen and college-aged years where her characters get knocked on their asses, torn inside out, and put back together again by their first loves. Whether it's in a fantastical setting where human guards protect the creatures of the night or a realistic high school backdrop where social cliques rule the halls, the emotions are the same. Dark. Twisty. Angsty. Raw.

When Erin's not writing, you can find her dreaming up vacations for her family, watching murder mystery shows, or dancing in her kitchen while she pretends to cook.

Made in United States
Orlando, FL
03 December 2023